Gnosis
Legacy War Book 1

John Walker

DISCLAIMER

This is a work of fiction. Names, characters, business, places, events, and incidents are either the products of the author's imagination or used in a fictitious manner. Any resemblance to actual persons, living or dead, or actual events is purely coincidental. This story contains explicit language and violence.

Blurb

A Surprise attack.

Technology has allowed humanity to take to the stars. Earth's first step toward exploring the unknown universe begins with a surge of hope followed by the sting of a surprise attack. Just as their most advanced ship embarks on its maiden voyage, aliens assault the unprepared fleet, making a play for an ancient technology the human race has relied upon for all major advances.

This sudden meeting proves humans are not the only sentient beings in the vastness of space and it quickly becomes clear they will need to thwart the plans of their new enemies. If they do not, our first foray into the unknown could well be our last.

Chapter 1

Captain Desmond Bradford leaned forward, willing the ship to move faster. They had received reports of the attack less than twenty minutes earlier and were well on their way back to Earth. Hyperspace made distances meaningless but travel was not instantaneous. The maiden voyage of the Gnosis took them to the edge of the solar system.

Another ten minutes would see them return home.

Experience told him every second counted when it came to combat and the defense force needed them. Though the other ships were certainly capable, the Gnosis was the most powerful ship in the fleet. The best experimental technology made up the offensive and defensive capabilities of the vessel, making it ideal for the intended purpose of exploration.

And just on the verge of our first trip, an unknown enemy force attacks Earth. Desmond narrowed his eyes. Who could it be? The unification put the old conflicts to rest a long time ago. They can't possibly be gunning for the Orb ... can they?

The view screen showed the glowing yellow-green pulse light of hyperspace. Faster-than-light travel made for an incredible light show as they rocketed through what scientists call an alternate dimension. An intense, focused burst of energy allowed them to enter then hurtle themselves well beyond the speed of light.

"Sixty seconds to destination," Lieutenant Salina Gold announced from the science station. She wore her brown hair in a tight bun, her face set in a neutral, professional expression. "Scan data coming through now. Enemy ships number ten and are hitting orbital defenses as well as the fleet."

"Thank you," Desmond said. He turned to Commander Vincent Bowman sitting to his right. His first officer's blue eyes were narrowed in concentration, his nearly shaved blond hair spiking in the middle of his head. "Who do you think we're racing to fight?"

"Can't say," Vincent replied. "Maybe some fringe from the Eastern Coalition? But where would they get the equipment? Anything capable of standing against our defenses would need some serious tech. Stolen maybe?"

Desmond shook his head. "I didn't hear anything about missing gear in any briefing I've attended."

"We're about to find out one way or another." Vincent shrugged. "I hope we're ready."

"Emerging from hyperspace now, sir." Salina called. "Control transferring to Lieutenant Commander Caplan in five … four … three … two … one …"

As the light show faded and they emerged into normal space, a chaotic battle raged dead ahead. Ships from the Earth fleet clashed with unusual vessels unlike any Desmond had ever seen. He gestured to Salina but he knew she was already performing a full scan of their opponents.

Lieutenant Commander Zachary Caplan was the ship's pilot and one of the best in the fleet. He could've been Vincent's brother with his light hair and blue eyes though he was a bit shorter and more slight. He'd been a fighter pilot before moving into the helmsman station and his flying instincts served him well in the new role.

"Permission to engage?" Zach asked, hands poised to follow the order. Desmond would've preferred to wait for some more intel but the fleet's SOS made it clear they needed help immediately. The Gnosis had to get in the fight immediately or risk losing good men and women.

"Granted," Desmond said. "Close to range and target the closest enemy. Be nimble though. When the scans complete, we may need to change up our tactics."

"Captain," Salina spoke up quickly. "I'm picking up odd readings from the hulls of these ships. They have shields, like ours, but theirs are deflecting my ability to receive system information. I highly recommend we use beam weapons to disrupt their defenses before employing our mass drivers."

Desmond watched the screen as the enemy ships fired blue beams at the Earth fleet. The weapons caused their shields to light up but didn't immediately pierce them. Wherever they came from, they weren't giants so it gave him some faith that they'd be able to fend them off. However, they clearly came with some advantages if they could deflect scans.

The attackers numbered at twelve large ships, each one holding their own against two to one odds with the Earth fleet. At first glance, it appeared the fight might be even but it only took a few moments to see the invaders had an advantage. They were soaking incoming shots and dishing out a nearly continuous assault.

The ship rumbled and he turned to Salina again. Her hands flew over the controls at her panel, the touch screen causing a quiet, dull thump with every finger stroke. "We just experienced the wake of a stray attack. None of the enemy ships have engaged us as of yet. They are too occupied with the fleet."

"Hit them, Zach," Desmond said. "Fire at will. Draw their fire away from our allies."

The Gnosis had the best defenses in the fleet. While they didn't know what to expect from the attacks of their enemies, Desmond knew they could weather a direct assault for longer. As they rapidly approached the fray, he sat back down and braced himself for what came next. He was about to conduct a major battle in an untested ship with a crew that had worked together for barely six months.

Thank God everyone's well trained.

The deck trembled slightly as Zach fired the beam weapons. Orange light lanced forward and struck one of the targets, slamming them hard enough to penetrate their defenses and cause the hull to spark. Desmond hadn't anticipated their attack being so successful immediately. Everything he had studied about shields suggested they should've repelled the strike.

"They have fighters," Salina said. "I'm picking up smaller vessels attacking our orbital defense systems."

"Vincent, how long to deploy interceptors?"

Vincent checked his computer before replying. "Our pilots were standing by from when we got the distress call. Hangar control reports they can be out there in less than two minutes."

"Launch when ready." Desmond gestured to the screen, redirecting his focus. "Hit that same target with the mass drivers before they can retaliate."

Mass drivers threw chunks of metal, propelling them at hypersonic speed. As a barrage battered the hull of the enemy, pieces of the target began to break off and sail into space. The vessel popped a moment later, destroyed from their attacks.

"Okay, we can handle these guys," Desmond said. "Zach, acquire your next target and fire. Salina, do you have a full scan of what they're putting out?"

"They have a similar energy signature to our own," Salina replied. "I suspect we hit one which diverted power to weapons. We may not have as easy a time with other ships in their fleet. And the fighters are also quite advanced. I advise caution to our own pilots. They'll want to fly defensively I suspect, at least until they fully understand the capabilities of their opponents."

"Vincent, convey that to our pilots," Desmond said, "and provide command oversight throughout the engagement there. I want them away from our orbital defenses. I'll take care of the capital ship situation."

"The orbital defenses are firing back," Salina announced. "But they seem to be unable to calculate proper lead to hit the smaller ships."

"Something to keep in mind as we do a retrospective on this fight," Desmond replied. "Zach, time to next target."

Zach hummed. "Five seconds ... and we'll be in range of several of them at that point."

"Keep your targeting tight," Desmond said. "We'll move through them as quickly as we can but getting them from two angles should definitely tip the scales. Salina, have you been in contact with our people yet? Did anyone try to talk before this broke out? Or was it a total sneak attack?"

"No communication occurred before the attack," Salina reported. "They emerged from hyperspace near the moon, closed the distance and fired. Their initial entry gave our fleet time to intercept. We received the distress call the moment the enemy showed up and began ignoring hails."

"Which is why we were here right when it started," Desmond said. "Thank you. Vincent, report on fighters?"

"Mustang Squadron is our first response unit. Raptor's up next and will cover them." Vincent tapped his screen before continuing. "We're holding bomber units in reserve at this time."

"They shouldn't be needed." Desmond watched as they fired their beam weapons again. This time, the enemy's shields held firm. He nodded. Salina was right, and they figured it out quickly too. They know we're hitting them with some heavy ordnance and they also have the means to defend against it. This fight won't be as cut and dry as I hoped. "Keep it up, Zach."

The enemy ship disengaged from the Earth fleet to put more attention on the Gnosis. As it tried to acquire a firing solution, Zach fired again, this time doubling up energy blasts with a mass driver barrage. The two together caused superficial damage but enough to give the Earth fleet some confidence.

A beam weapon struck the Gnosis in the bow, making the shields flash bright enough to make the screen go temporarily white. Desmond winced and turned to Salina, waiting for her report on their defenses. She shook her head, not bothering to look up to offer her analysis. "Defenses held. Shield power drained to eighty percent in that one blast. Recharging now."

If they concentrated their fire, they could be dangerous. Especially if they hit a single point. Desmond nodded and let Zach do his job, returning fire again. The brawl might last longer than they wanted and he needed to start thinking of alternative tactics rather than keep exchanging fire. Maybe they'd need the bombers after all.

"I'm receiving a message from high command," Salina said. "They are …" She went silent, drawing Desmond's attention.

"What is it?"

"The aliens have attacked Gamma Alpha."

Desmond's stomach flipped at the thought. Gamma Alpha might've been the single most well defended structure on the entire planet. It held the Orb and though plenty of potential intruders attempted to access the base, they all failed. Could they repel whoever these invaders were? It really depended on their weapons … and how many they sent.

"They are requesting help from us," Salina said. "From our expeditionary troops."

Desmond nodded. "Get them on a shuttle and have Raptor escort them through this mess. If they're asking for help, that's not good."

I've been to Gamma Alpha. The gun emplacements alone should be enough to drive any ground force off. What did they bring to get through there? I guess we'll find out soon enough. This orbital attack might be a ruse to get what they want down there. I guess we're fighting a battle on three fronts. Time to earn our pay.

***

Squadron Leader Dennis Arden launched first, providing what he hoped to be solid leadership to the rest of his Mustang unit. They'd trained together, flying simulations and formation work for the past six months, but none of them had seen actual combat as a team. Today, they would be tested.

Some of them had fought in earlier conflicts with inferior technology with different units. Dennis brawled with separatists over Australia when he'd been out of flight school for less than a month. Back then, they kept things mostly in atmosphere against opponents they easily understood, other human beings with similar equipment.

The briefing for this fight stated they would be taking on what command believed to be alien invaders. Their ships certainly didn't match the Earth variety. Checking his scanner, he brought up the silhouettes. Rounded with a thorn like protrusion on one side and thrusters opposite it, they appeared to be highly maneuverable and quick.

In contrast, the interceptors Dennis and his squadron flew went with a variable swept wing approach to allow for trans-atmospheric flight. They could tuck them in during especially tight maneuvering and their weapons came from the stubby nose or the body itself. Three thrusters provided rear propulsion and dozens of micro thrusters gave them their alternative motion.

The other five came out behind him, forming up in a wide vanguard. Their orders were to help defend the orbital defense systems, which weren't able to keep up with the smaller attackers. Commander Bowman told them to observe prior to attack, giving them a warning about the advanced technology they might be facing.

Dennis did so on their way to the operational theater, altering his attention between his scanner's high resolution images and the path directly in front of him. The enemies were fast and maneuverable, climbing and banking around energy blasts that might've destroyed them with a single shot if they became careless.

Speaking of which, we need to have the orbital defenses settle down when we're in range. I don't want to have a friendly fire incident.

He tried to ping orbital defense control but an error appeared on his screen, some kind of low level interference. Redirecting his signal back to the ship, he got through but not without a liberal amount of static. "This is Mustang One to Gnosis Control. Can you boost your gain? The connection out here is terrible."

"This is Commander Bowman. We'll do what we can from here."

"Thank you, sir. I can't reach Orbital either. Can you make sure they crank down when we get there?"

"Friend or foe should be active," Commander Bowman replied. "We'll do what we can from here though. Time to engagement?"

"Um …" Dennis glanced at the scanner and frowned. "They're coming our way." An energy beam flew past his cockpit and he jogged to the right, putting a little more distance from it. His heart beat a little faster but he maintained his composure, and replied in an even tone, "Contact. Enemy has engaged."

"Fire at will," Commander Bowman said. "Repeat, fire at will."

Dennis signaled the rest of his squadron just as more shots grazed his shields. He initiated evasive maneuvers, spinning and falling into a dive. His wingman, Flight Lieutenant Shane Goring followed suit as the rest of his unit broke off into pairs. The fight kicked into high gear, energy beams lighting up the space all around them.

The targeting computer failed to secure a connection with the enemy ships. Scans indicated they were giving off some kind of radiation, a field interfering with the connection. "We're doing this the old fashioned way, folks." Dennis spoke over the com. "Save your missiles and stick to guns and beams. You'll probably have to get pretty damn close."

"Yeah, I can't get a lock," Shane said. "You think that's part of their defenses?"

"Doesn't matter," Lieutenant Hal Brown, Mustang Three, called out. "My computer can't get through it. I'm engaging."

Dennis glanced to the right and saw his ally make an attack run with Lieutenant Kate Zeller, his wingman, close behind. They both strafed their target, blasting away with mass driver cannons before pulling up and away, parting at the last second. A blue field erupted around their opponent, shields taking direct damage before fading back to a dull haze.

Shane began firing, throttling up to overtake him. His attack made the enemy pull up and rocket off and Dennis maneuvered to follow. He fell in behind his target's thrusters, blue ovals that made a fantastic focus. They tried to shake him, moving to the left and right but he timed it, firing a blast to get his bearings.

A clean miss gave him some perspective and he tilted the stick for a better shot. As the enemy continued its pendulum-like motion, he fired again, this time scoring a direct hit. The mass drivers pounded the shields and nudged the ship enough to break its motion cycle. He fired his beams this time, holding down the trigger and sweeping to the left.

The attack cut across his focus, blasting the shields and making them shatter like energized glass. Shane followed up with mass drivers and with nothing to stop them, the enemy engines were annihilated. The pilot ejected, his pod hurtling off into space but they didn't have time to worry about it. Two more invaders engaged them and they had to go defensive again.

Mustang five and six called out their own adventure as they buzzed one of the orbital defenses, buying themselves some distance before spinning around and taking another ship out. Hal called a mayday but before they could even get a fix on his position, he shouted into the microphone. "I've been hit! Direct hit! Ejecting! Ejecting!"

Λ massive explosion brightened Dennis's cockpit to the left and he looked over just in time to see the bits of Hal's ship go flying into nothingness. "Form up, people! Gnosis Control, where the hell is Raptor? This is crazy out here."

"They're escorting drop shuttles," Commander Bowman said. "Do your best until they get back."

"Escorting ..." Dennis shook his head. "What for? Where?"

"Enemy forces are attacking Gamma Alpha." Dennis's heart nearly stopped when he received the news. "We're sending troops down to stop them."

"Understood." Dennis sighed. "You heard that, everyone. We have to make this happen. Remain evasive and take shots as you can. Opportunities will present themselves but take risks sparingly. Our first mission should not be our last."

Another set of enemy ships took shots at them, smacking the shields hard. Dennis's ship shook and an alarm went off. Automated repair systems kicked in and rerouted power as necessary. He spun to the right and fired blind, hoping a random act might make them break off. It seemed to work because another assault didn't come.

One of the orbital defenses exploded, adding to the overall chaos of the scene. All of Mustang reformed, staying far enough apart to avoid splash damage from an incoming attack. This presented the enemy with an opportunity Dennis hoped they'd take and as three ships came around to take on their tail, he ordered Mustang Four and Five to dive and attack.

The two ships went down while the other three pulled up. They spun around and met the enemy as they attempted their own evasive maneuvers. More attacks filled space, a wild melee breaking out between all the ships. There was enough ordnance floating around to make standard visual almost impossible.

Something blew nearby and Dennis prayed it wasn't one of his people.

"Target eliminated," Flying Officer Alicia Quinn, Mustang Five, announced. "The other two are falling back and we've got three on Orbital Satellite Seven."

"Let's get over there and drive them off," Dennis said. "It's more important we keep those alive than fighting these jerks."

They redirected their course, advancing to full speed. The magnetic inertial dampeners made the transition easy on the body but there was still enough gravitational pressure to make Dennis know they were really hauling ass. As they closed the distance, the satellite came into view and continued to grow as they approached.

The stationary weapons fired wildly but continued to miss. The enemy proved too agile to take down. Dennis fired as soon as he was remotely in range and he nicked his target in the tail. This caused the opponent to redirect and fly straight toward him. Great, chicken time. Dennis fired the mass drivers even as his foe let loose with energy beams.

They hit each other but the mass drivers won this round. The enemy shields faltered and the nose took a direct blow, shattering the metal and causing it to spin before the engines ignited and tore the entire hull apart. Dennis dove to avoid the debris but he didn't quite escape every chunk. Some pieces burned up when tapping his shields.

"Careful with risks, huh?" Shane chuckled. "That looked pretty damn risky to me."

"Yeah, I'm not smart," Dennis replied. "So sue me. Get back in it."

Another ship went down as Kate blasted away, tearing through the side of the shields and taking it apart. A panel popped off the enemy and slammed into her underbelly, causing her to spin for a moment before she regained control. "I'm okay," she announced. "Minimal concussion damage. Automated systems are correcting now. Real combat's taking a bit to get used to."

Capital ships moved in their direction and Dennis knew if they had to engage those big guys, they'd be in a lot of trouble. The enemy had the advantage of defying their target locks. He doubted they suffered the same restriction. "We might need some bombers out here."

Shane took out the final of three ships that were attacking the orbital defense satellite. "Why? We've got the hard points here. They can repel those jerks."

"I kinda doubt it." Dennis scowled, looking for their next targets. "Looks like we've got some fighters moving on the Gnosis. Home base has better things to do than play with a bunch of gnats so follow me and prepare to engage. I want to clear that up before we move on to anything else."

He sent a waypoint to the others and once again accelerated to full throttle. They needed to get back there quickly if they hoped to make any difference in that particular fight. Already, they'd managed to put a dent in the enemy's assault. Providing they got Hal back with a search and rescue, they might even be able to call their battle successful.

But they had a long way to go before they could call it won.

***

Gunnery Sergeant Geoff Heathrow sat near the pilots in the shuttle as it made its way for Earth. Their escorts remained close enough to make out every detail of their frames just outside the window but they didn't seem to be needed. The mainstay of the enemy force fought over the orbital defenses and the Gnosis kept the bigger ships busy.

Getting there won't be the problem. What will we find when we arrive?

Communications with the surface were spotty due to some kind of powerful interference. The intelligence they had simply suggested an unknown force had attacked Gamma Alpha, where the Orb was kept. Orders came through suggesting surface security specifically requested a unit from the Gnosis should arrive and assist.

Geoff had been in the military for the better part of fifteen years. He applied for a ride on the Gnosis as soon as the post opened up and looked forward to the crazy stuff they'd discover. He liked the idea of exploration and understood the need for security in such situations. It seemed like they'd put war behind them a long time ago.

I guess someone had some other ideas about that. I hope this is an isolated incident.

"Heat!" Sergeant Lawrence Gorman called out. When Geoff joined up, his drill instructor shortened his surname, creating a lifelong handle that followed him to every post. "I'm still not getting through the interference for scans. We're going in blind here. Any thoughts on what we might expect?"

The truth was simple. Heat had no idea what they were going to find down there other than a force large enough to drive back the security unit. If they were inside the base, automated defenses should've been slowing them down. He'd seen them in action, at least simulated, and no ground force should've been able to stand against them.

"I'm worried about their technology," Heat said. "But our stuff is pretty good too. I imagine we're going to have a sweep and clear situation then go home."

"You think this might be an invasion?" Sergeant Alex Gillet asked. "An expeditionary force to test our defenses?"

"Seems to me they're after the Orb," Heat replied. "And if that's so, they didn't bring enough people because we're not letting them have it. We're breaking up into groups of three. Me, Gillet and Anderson are

Sentinel One. Gorman, Dorian and Wheeler are two. Vine, Bosh and Kelly are three. You got it?"

The men all shouted out an affirmative and Heat returned to looking over his HUD, controlling it with the touch pad built into his glove. Their armor was power assisted, granting them the benefits of hydraulics for heavy lifting and even some pretty impressive jumps. Assisted by rocket packs, they could cover ground quickly, especially difficult terrain.

They carried heavy weapons, easily capable of puncturing armored transports or offensive vehicles like tanks. Each man also packed a couple of small missiles for taking out air threats. If there were something on the planet they weren't prepared for, the situation would prove far more dire than they could handle on their own.

Heat put in a request for Raptor to remain as air support should they need it. The squadron leader replied an affirmative and they committed to flying the perimeter, ensuring no other enemies came in to flank them. This would afford the soldiers a little breathing room and allow them to concentrate on the threat immediately in front of them.

The shuttle hit the atmosphere hard, piercing their re-entry window and plunging toward the surface. Panels rattled around them and the seats bucked. The safety harness held him in place, clinging tightly to the armor. It held him in place but didn't lessen the discomfort of the descent.

Getting there will be half the fun in this case. At least all we have to deal with here is being shaken. Once we're on the surface, the real fun begins and we get to test these fancy new weapons in a live combat exercise. I'd hoped for something more subtle for our first time out. Oh well.

"Thirty seconds." The pilot spoke in an even, bored tone over the com. He was referring to the time it would take to drop them off roughly two hundred feet above the ground. They would use their jump packs to safely land and approach the base. Each of them practiced the tactic hundreds of times but never while being shot at, not with live ammo at least.

Gorman and Dorian stood and released the safety mechanisms holding the ramp in place. They counted out ten before popping the hatch. The wind made the straps dance around but Heat's helmet cancelled out the noise. The rest of the men stood and prepared for the jump. Single file, they got the green light and started jumping.

Heat took up the rear, hopping out after the others. The rest of the unit looked like gray dots against white clouds. His HUD showed his altitude and it plunged, the number spinning wildly as it counted down toward zero. He knew the cloud coverage should clear up in less than five seconds then they'd be getting rained on.

The computer stated the storm would likely pass before the hour was up. Hopefully, we'll be done with this mission by then.

All at once the clouds were gone and he saw Gamma Alpha. The facility itself was not overly large on the outside. Just a set of cement walls, barracks, automated defenses and a command center. Most of it was beneath the ground and built into the mountain. People worked and lived inside, studying the Orb and protecting it.

Heat saw orange-beam weapons firing from the Earth defenses as the enemy returned blue shots. His heartbeat picked up at the thought of combat, of getting into the action and taking them on. The coms cleared up a moment later and Gamma Alpha control sent out a wild mayday, the operator practically screaming.

"We hear you," Heat said. "We're almost there. What's the sitrep?"

"We're holding some of the invaders outside but at least three of them got through our defenses and are in the base. Our soldiers are struggling to push them back!"

"So you don't need us at the front gate," Heat replied. "You want us inside ASAP?"

"Yes, sir. Can you get through quickly?"

"Absolutely and we've got enough to help outside. Your corridors are too tight for all of us anyway." Some of his men landed already and took up positions. Heat hit his pack and he slowed immediately, his body jostled by the sudden thrust. He landed in a crouch, weapon aimed outward.

They formed up and started toward the base and he gave them the briefing. He would lead Gillet and Anderson into the base. The others would tear through the remaining enemies outside. When he gave the order, the other six sprang into action, using their jets to cover the ground faster.

The enemy combatants were humanoid, perhaps a trifle taller than the average human. They wore some type of armor, blue in color and it shimmered. Scans indicated some kind of personal shield, something which might afford them one or two shots before they had to rely solely on the physical protection.

Sentinel Three plunged into the fight and started blasting away, firing their own beam weapons at the enemy from behind. The first one to take a hit stumbled forward, dropping to one knee. His shield saved his life but the next two shots, concentrated fire from multiple troops, cut through his armor and obliterated everything from the shoulders up.

That caused the invaders to fight their battle on two fronts, half their contingent turning to battle Sentinel Two and Three. As Heat and his party jumped toward the entrance, he noted a number of bodies littering the ground. Twenty invaders mingled with perhaps forty humans. His scans indicated a few survived but they wouldn't for long, not even with medical attention.

What a mess.

They landed with a resounding crash just before the entrance, the doors smashed and lying on the ground several feet inside. Small guns smoked nearby and the cameras were also down. Heat readied his weapon and headed within, relying on his HUD to collect some intelligence data.

A few feet inside, a red light flashed in his helmet. He directed his attention to what could be causing it and found a system alert. The aliens were closing in on the final defenses of the Orb. Only three doors stood between them and the ultimate prize on Earth. Heat motioned for his men to double time it.

Their armor clashed with the metal floor, making a massive racket. The enemy would hear them coming but they didn't have time for stealth. Besides, calling Heat's crew in meant someone wanted a loud solution to a pressing problem. As they rounded a corner and passed by the bodies of defenders and the debris of broken defenses, anger began to build.

After the initial discovery of the Orb, several nations threatened to fight over what it represented and what it offered. Ultimately, the violence that nearly occurred brought them together. There was too much work for any one organization to accomplish alone. Collaboration advanced humanity by light years.

And now someone's coming to collect on a bill it seems.

Heat's HUD indicated violence up ahead. They paused at the corner and stacked up. When they stepped out into the hallway, they'd have full line of sight on five targets. Two of them were attempting to bypass the security with some kind of device. The others stood guard with their weapons held at the ready.

"Ready on three." Heat spoke into his com. Noise suppressors kept his voice from carrying and as he counted down, he saw the other two tense up for the fight. None of them knew precisely what would happen if they were shot by the enemy's weapons. The unknown made the situation that much more intense. "Three … two … one."

The men darted out from their cover, leading with their weapons. Their targets were only startled for half a moment before the shooting began. Heat's first shot struck one of the enemies in the leg, causing him to stumble backward. The alien's attack went wide, striking the ceiling and causing sparks to rain down from a broken light fixture.

Gillet took a shot to the chest. His armor held but the impact of the blow made him lose his balance. He dropped to one knee and fired his jump jet, a quick burst to keep him aloft. The gesture kept him from falling but he overshot and slammed into the ceiling, firing at the same time. The shot went wide but it grazed one of the aliens trying to get through the door.

A moment of chaos broke out as the aliens tried to take evasive action, preserving themselves for another few moments in the midst of the violence. As the conflict continued, Heat took three more shots, one to the shoulder, another to the leg and a final blow to his chest. The HUD showed minimal damage, the technology proving its worth.

"Incoming grenade!" Anderson shouted, firing his jets to hop backwards. Heat made a split second decision, realizing he'd very likely run into one of his allies if he followed suit. Dashing forward, he jammed the thrusters on and slammed into one of the aliens, taking him straight into the wall.

The body collapsed beneath the weight and momentum of his armor and as he moved away, the broken corpse slid to the floor. The explosion made him drop to his knees and he spun in place, ready to fire again. Gillet caught one of the targets in the head and the final one threw up his arms in surrender, his gun flying through the air.

"Station Two, this is Sentinel One," Heat said. "We've secured the area and have a prisoner, please respond."

"Sentinel One, this is two," Gorman replied. "All enemies neutralized and mop up complete. We are policing the bodies and preparing for a post op. Over."

"Good work. Get in touch with Gamma Alpha control and let them know we're ready to turn this place back over to them." Heat paused. "And we'll need some serious clean up down here."

"Affirmative, sir. Sentinel two out."

***

□

Chapter 2

Desmond grabbed his chair to steady himself as enemy fire battered their shields. Salina called out that they had dropped down to thirty percent and started recharging. They'd been brawling with several of the enemies, exchanging shots and while the Gnosis proved to have a distinct advantage, the sheer number of vessels they stood against evened the odds.

"We've got a massive power surge from the marked alien vessel," Salina said. "I recommend a withdraw."

"Fall back," Desmond ordered. Zach slapped his controls and the ship lurched as it moved away. A bright blue flash filled the screen, moving in a sphere around the target. It bathed several of the Earth ships. Sparks danced away from each craft the field touched and their shields flared in a rainbow of colors.

When it touched the Gnosis, they were fairly far back. The ship lights dimmed briefly and came back firm. When the rumbling stopped, Desmond pointed at the screen. "Get us back in the action, Zach. Fire when ready but keep an eye on energy bursts. We'll need to pull away quickly if that happens again. Salina, damage report."

Salina hummed. "Aft thrusters require minor repairs from electrical shorts. All other systems are holding firm. Shields blocked the energy wave but they were drained. We're at thirty percent and charging fast. While we made it through with minimal impact, the fleet did not. I'm getting a com message about two of them abandoning ship."

"Damn." Desmond checked his own screen to see the rest. More than twelve enemies started the fight and they were now down to four. Earth lost two of their own and reports came in about extensive damage from the assault. He frowned as he read through the information. He needed a confirmation. "Why didn't the enemy take damage from their attack?"

"I can only speculate," Salina replied. "Their defenses are likely matched up to the energy field so when it bursts as it did, they absorb the attack and possibly even overpower their shields temporarily. Further analysis will be required and it looks like we'll have plenty of debris to make the investigation easier."

Desmond nodded. "How many are combat effective still?"

"Three, including the one we just hit." Salina brought up a second image on the main view screen, a shot of a massive ordnance exchange. They watched as three Earth ships hammered one of the enemies, tearing through their shields and penetrating the hull. The ship went up a moment later. "Make that two."

Zach tapped his controls and called out, "I've targeted the one who did that sphere thing. Firing now."

The mass drivers popped off several rounds but the beams got there first, cutting into their shields. Each blow knocked them down just a little until the chunks of metal arrived to batter them like ancient rams in some castle siege. He immediately fired again and the second barrage tore through their shields.

They initiated their engines and tried to move off but it was too late to flee. Their engines were taken down a moment later and they began to drift. Desmond moved over to Salina's station and checked the scans, noting a different kind of power surge building in the enemy's hull. They weren't about to attack. Something was blowing up.

"They've had a power failure," Salina said. "Look ..."

The ship burst like a balloon, pieces flying off in different directions. Some of the debris burned up in the atmosphere, the larger pieces glowing bright enough to be easily seen on screen.

Their last two ships tried to depart but the maneuverable Earth fleet gave chase. Desmond ordered Zach to follow as well though he knew full well they wouldn't get far. "Open a channel and hail these guys. Maybe we can get them to stand down and surrender. Also, where are we at with our fighters?"

"Orbital defenses are secure," Vincent said. "They engaged a small group of fighters en route to us a few minutes ago. They're taking care of them right now."

Salina spoke up. "No response on any channel, sir."

"They don't want to surrender," Zach said. "Escape or die, they're going for one or the other."

"I'd like to know why they even thought they could take us with such a small contingency," Vincent said. "Did they not know our military capabilities?"

"Technically speaking," Salina said, "they would've overwhelmed our fleet in a few minutes without our support. And the report I've received from Gamma Alpha suggests the aliens were able to breach the station and nearly made it to the Orb. Though our ships and defenses worked admirably, without us this could've been a catastrophe."

"And it still wasn't good," Desmond replied. He watched as they performed concentrated fire on the last two ships. Hitting them with everything they had, the first one was taken down almost instantly. The last one went up all on its own, a clear suicide rather than risk being caught. "Fantastic. No one to question about this senseless attack."

"Untrue, sir," Salina said. "Sentinel One reports they have a prisoner."

"Seriously?" Vincent looked up. "That's great news! Right?"

Desmond nodded. "Language barrier aside, that's better than we had a few moments ago. How're the fighters doing?"

"They've mopped up, sir," Vincent said. "When the larger enemy ships started to make a break for it, the fighters tried to escape. Showing our guys their tailpipes wasn't a good idea."

"Good. Let's get some search and rescue going." Desmond returned to his seat, leaning forward. "Get us in orbit, Zach. I have a feeling we'll be here for a while. Launch shuttle teams when ready."

"Captain," Salina said, "I've got high command on the com. They'd like to talk to you right away."

"Is it private?"

"No, sir."

"Put them on screen."

Admiral Garlan Reach was an older man in his sixties, with thin and close-cropped gray hair. His blue eyes were nearly gray and the lines on his face were just as much a testament to his career as the ribbons on his chest or the medals he wore beside them. His grave expression shifted to a slightly more friendly visage, a thin smile touching his lips.

"I'm glad you got back in time, Desmond. Thanks for the rush."

"The hyperspace trip back provided us an opportunity to test the system under stress," Desmond said. "Much as I wish we didn't have to find out, real combat for my people may not have been on the dance card but we at least know the systems work now. How're things at Gamma Alpha? I guess our soldiers were able to get things in order."

"Those aliens were able to tear through our defenses pretty well. Even when we were holding them, their technology … It seemed to be capable of negating some of our most advanced weapons. We've captured a great deal of it and will be analyzing it as quickly as possible. That's why I've contacted you."

Desmond's brows lifted. "Okay … what do you need me to do, sir?"

"I'd like you to come down here as soon as possible. We've got a lot to talk about." Garlan cleared his throat. "An agent from the AIA just arrived a few moments ago to help with this situation. Apparently, the moment our defenses were breached, they were alerted."

"How's that?"

"I don't know." Garlan scowled. "However, I intend to find out. Just get down here as quickly as you can and we'll get to the bottom of this situation. Admiral Reach out."

The screen went back to space and Desmond leaned back in his chair with a deep breath. The AIA stood for Applied Intelligence Association, a group that didn't really advertise precisely what they did. They rarely got involved in the affairs of the military, at least not overtly or to Desmond's knowledge. Whatever caught their interest about this encounter must've been big.

The Gnosis performed well during the fight and with minimal damage, Engineer Nathaniel Webber would easily get them back to normal in a few hours. Their enemy's weapons concerned Desmond far more. The strange sphere and even their beam weapons were particularly nasty. Concentrated, they might've caused real damage to the ship.

They came thinking they'd get an easy fight and they attacked while we were pretty far away. Were they just waiting for their chance? Did they know we might be capable of stopping them? And what were their motivations in the first place? Why even bother to attack a whole planet with so few ships?

The prisoner would be able to answer these questions if they could communicate with him. Perhaps that's why the AIA was involved. They might have methods to talk to the guy regardless of what language he spoke. Rumors about that organization ranged from the extraordinary to the absurd.

Desmond stood and gestured at Vincent. "You have the bridge, Commander. Salina, contact Lieutenant Quinn and have him relieve you. I'd like you to join me on the surface. Keep the search and rescue going and contact me if you have any problems. We'll be back soon."

Hopefully with answers. No one's going to feel safe if we don't figure out the motivations of these invaders, and will this lead to something far worse than a skirmish? Lord knows we don't need another war.

***

Dennis and the rest of Mustang Squadron remained in the field until search and rescue located Hal's escape pod. They escorted the shuttle back to the Gnosis and landed at that point. When they disembarked, they found their squad mate took some bruises but otherwise made it out unscathed.

Thank God for small favors. They lingered around the medical bay, waiting for a debriefing order to come through. Shane leaned against the wall, hand pressed against his ear to listen to com traffic. He tilted his head and turned to the others. "I've got something interesting. Seems the captain is heading down to Gamma Alpha."

"Did they get that mess cleaned up?" Kate asked. "Or did he have to go down there himself to get those jar heads in line?"

Shane smirked. "They stopped the force trying to bust in, if that's what you're asking. Raptor's escorting his shuttle down to the surface now."

"Glad we didn't end up on milk run duty," Flying Office Corey Parks said. "I didn't sign up to follow around slow ass shuttles."

Dennis rolled his eyes before replying, "You signed up to do as you're told but off the record, I'm glad we didn't pull that duty. Of course, it's a necessary service. VIPs need protection."

"Those aliens," Shane said, shaking his head, "they were after the Orb. If they got it ... imagine what they would do to our technological race."

"We've got some backups," Corey said. "From what I heard, we've been trying to copy data off the thing for a while."

"Yeah, but it's not exactly easy," Kate replied. "They said the storage capacity of the Orb is impossibly large. Copying it has also proven to be a challenge so people have to transcribe it. That's why it's so valuable and why we couldn't let it fall into enemy hands."

"You get anything else on the com?" Dennis asked. "Or are we done?"

Shane shrugged. "Just that Admiral Reach will be meeting them down there. Must be serious to bring out a guy like that."

"No doubt." Corey paced away, rubbing his chin. "Think we'll see some more action then?"

"Those guys weren't alone," Dennis said. "There're more of them somewhere and we'll have to be ready. I doubt they're giving up because we bloodied their nose once."

"War then," Flying Officer Alicia Quinn added. "We'll be at war again."

The comment silenced the ground but Dennis nodded in response. All of them thought about it but she was the only one to voice the concern. Whatever happened in the next few hours might mean the difference between digging in for a defensive run or heading out into the unknown reaches of space for a hunting expedition.

One way or another, the Gnosis would see some action soon. Dennis felt he and his team were ready.

***

Cassandra Alexander hated wearing her intelligence uniform. The white jacket slacks combo made her feel like an uptight socialite and the heeled shoes didn't suit her. She'd always been far more practical about her clothing and in that getup, she didn't dare touch any food or drink other than water.

The thin blouse beneath didn't provide enough padding between her skin and coat, making her shoulders and back itch. Wearing her dark hair in a tight bun, she looked like a woman ten years older when she peered into the mirror. At thirty-two, she did not enjoy the maturity of the look.

At least the assignment appealed to her. Gamma Alpha tended to be off limits to everyone and she'd only visited the Orb three times in the last six years. Each time required special permission and a couple escorts. Even as one of the foremost intelligence researchers of the data inherent in the device, she was expected to remotely access it.

Which proved to be just as good in most cases.

The AIA helped with some of the systems on the experimental Gnosis vessel. Cassie provided the programming driving the computer systems and helped to direct how it interacted with the automatic repair and defense protocols. She hadn't known she was doing it until they asked her to look over the work but that was the nature of working for intelligence.

Everything's a secret until the very last possible moment.

Since finding out she worked on the Gnosis, she had been allowed to test the systems in simulation as well as deep dive better ways to do the programming next time. An update cycle was put into place and though she didn't build those packages, she got to approve them after viewing the testing information and speak to the workers involved.

The work may not have been what she expected when she left the elite Design Information academy in Geneva but it proved rewarding enough. Someone of her skill and graduation position could've walked out making an enormous salary at any of the tech firms around the world but the AIA appealed to her sense of human patriotism.

"Where else will you be allowed to make a huge difference for everyone? Do you really want to spend your entire life making gadgets for the wealthy? You should be doing important things and we want to help you get there. The caveats are you won't get as much money and you can't talk about your work but think of the personal satisfaction."

The rhetoric almost didn't work until they told her she would be allowed to work with data straight from the Orb. Everyone on Earth knew about the device but so few people had access to it, even peripherally. The temptation became very real. At school, they were allowed to use the 'educational' section put out by the Protectors and that was enough to pique her interest.

Full access to the Orb would've made her commit her first born and both kidneys to any project they wanted. The ability to develop and study that thing made her sign up and thus began a career she never dreamed possible. While Cassie had the mental fortitude and drive for technology, she wasn't the most physically imposing figure and the AIA had to change that.

Their training program took the better part of a year and taught her a variety of skills she never considered necessary for her future. Unarmed combat, firearms, flying and insurgency all came with the package. Even after she finished the initial education, she had classes for the next two years and practice runs every week.

After three years, they made sure she kept up with her physical routine and that she practiced the others rigorously. It meant her days basically started with exercise, moved into technology advancements and study then more physical practice, a little more work and a few hours off at night.

By the time she hit thirty, she considered herself to be quite dangerous and certainly ready for whatever terrifying threat the AIA needed her to be prepared for. Considering the harmony on the planet, she didn't know what they expected. Separatist movements rose and fell occasionally but they were put down by the military long before anyone else needed to worry.

When she got the call telling her to hop a shuttle to Gamma Alpha immediately and to wear the dress uniform, she thought she was being called in for a training exercise. On the way there, she learned about the attack through a standard briefing then watched a news video about the battle in orbit.

The Gnosis performed admirably as did the other technology coming off of it. Brilliant.

The various media outlets were hailing the Gnosis crew as heroes though they didn't mention the attack on Gamma Alpha. AIA officials covered that part up but Cassie had the combat statistics from the soldiers who used the power armor. The data showed they took direct hits from beam weapons and the operators survived.

We knew the armor would make it but concussion was hard to judge. Looking at these figures, it appears they didn't even get injured. Fantastic.

Their battle caused extensive damage to one of the hallways leading to the Orb but at least that would be easy to fix.

I assume I'm here to determine why the aliens came after the Orb but the why is less obvious. Did they want to destroy it? Stealing it would've required more tools and equipment, more people. It's not exactly small. And there's no way they could've downloaded every bit of information in the thing. There's far too much.

The wonders of the Orb had yet to be fully exhausted so she admitted there was a good chance the aliens might have a way to scan through the thing in a more efficient manner than the interfaces setup by humanity. The fact they were dealing with a culture or species with knowledge of the device worried her more than the notion they were not alone in the universe.

The media will be playing up the angle of first contact for sure. They don't know how scary this really is. Not yet.

Cassie's com went off and she tapped it to answer without looking to see who it was. "Yes?"

"Miss Alexander," Jordan Bell spoke into the com, using the honorific Cassie disliked most. Would Ms kill him? He acted as the director of her division, not her direct lead but two above her in the rank ladder. "I hope you're en route to the facility already."

"I am," Cassie replied. "What can I do for you?"

"You'll be meeting with Captain Desmond Bradford of the Gnosis and his chief science officer Lieutenant Salina Gold. I've done some digging on both of them and can send you their dossiers if you'd like."

"Go ahead."

"Take a look before you land. The AIA is lending you out to the military for the duration of this operation."

Cassie's eyes widened. "Whoa, what does that mean exactly? What do you mean lending out? Am I a library book now?"

"You're one of the foremost experts not only on the Orb itself but much of the technology aboard their ship," Jordan said. "You're skills and talents are needed there. Furthermore, we need a representative in this situation and you're well trained and ready for such an assignment. I expect you are ready for some time off planet."

"With all due respect, I am not," Cassie replied. It took some effort to keep her voice even. "I was led to believe this was an advise and observe mission, not a full change of venue."

"Most of our assignments carry need to know points." Jordan smiled. "And you just now needed to know."

"I don't think it's funny."

"Just trying to soften the blow, Agent." Jordan sighed. "You'll have a chance to square your affairs at home before departing with the ship but I suspect you'll be heading out in the next few days. Good luck and let Andrea know if you have any other questions. She can make arrangements to have your things packed and your flat secured. Jordan out."

Cassie stared at her screen as the news occupied it again, numbers and letters flashing by unheeded. Jordan's news couldn't have surprised her more if he would've told her she'd be sent to mop the floors in an Amsterdam brothel. She didn't know if fear gripped her stomach or excitement. Despite the safety of a desk job, she did yearn to see something else.

Getting a chance to see the technology at work outside the simulations appealed to her. She took a deep breath to dispel the nerves working her over. Showing herself as jittery to a military commander wouldn't go over very well, especially if she was supposed to be taken seriously once they began working together.

The shuttle set down and she steadied herself one more time before disembarking. Military personnel rushed about the area, weapons at the ready. People to her left policed bodies and it made her stand up straighter. She'd seen dead bodies but never in a battlefield before, never recently killed.

What happened here? How did these aliens cause so much damage?

A young man in uniform approached. His shaved blond hair had been growing for maybe a week and his blue eyes made him look terribly young. He offered a salute but didn't look very certain. "Um … Miss Alexander?"

What is it with the Miss stuff? Cassie ignored the faux pas and smiled instead. "Yes. This is crazy."

"Yes, ma'am. They came from nowhere, hitting us hard. My name's Lieutenant Simon Walker. Please come with me." He stepped away from the platform and down the stairs. Cassie followed, really cursing the heels as they nearly got stuck in the grating of each step. "Are you here to help us analyze the attack data?"

"Um … something like that," Cassie replied. "I'm not entirely sure what I'm supposed to talk about yet. You understand."

"Yes, of course."

"Is it safe here?"

"Sentinel troops from the Gnosis came down and helped secure the area," Simon replied. "I have to say, we didn't know how they'd perform in that power armor. We heard rumors, sure, but seeing it in action? They came down here like angels of death er … I don't mean to sound like I'm using hyperbole, ma'am. But seriously, it was impressive."

"I'm sure it was." Cassie had seen videos of training simulations for the armor. They impressed her then and seeing the carnage, just imagining what they faced, improved her confidence in their technology. Practical application beats theory every day. "Where were you during the conflict?"

Simon gestured to one of the gun emplacements. "My crew manned that weapon. We were one of the lucky ones because the other turret was taken out by a high yield explosive. Melted the metal completely." He bowed his head for a moment. "We lost four people to that."

"I'm sorry to hear it." Cassie sighed. Thinking about the deaths dampened her excitement about the situation. Knowing their equipment worked didn't matter nearly as much as the lives they lost. Painful as it was, if they broke into a full-on war, many people would die. One of the best things to come from discovering the Orb was relative peace.

And instead of killing each other, something else has to show up and cause trouble.

They went up the stairs to the front of the facility and through the double doors usually meant for heavy equipment. The personnel doors seemed to be sealed off and guards protected each one. Cassie passed by two men in power armor who saluted Simon. They must've been from the Gnosis.

We'll have to outfit the standard guards here with this stuff now that it's been proven to work so efficiently. Early tests of the armor had some of the researchers convinced it might explode. The power cores on the devices were shielded but potentially unstable. They put them on meat covered dummies at first and moved them remotely, testing what they might do to a human body.

The first units did explode but they corrected the problem and continued trials. Eventually, the fourth-generation units were considered safe enough for humans to try out. After six months, the production version went live and those were the ones that boarded the Gnosis.

Simon escorted her down a bland, metal hallway and to a conference room located near the Orb control room. She'd been there plenty of times to observe and work with the peripheral interface but the device itself was kept much deeper into the facility. Somewhere down there, a fight broke out and the creatures trying to break in were killed.

I wonder who I'm meeting now.

The door opened and several people turned to look at her. She recognized them from dossiers. The older uniformed gentlemen at the head of the table was Admiral Reach, in charge of military operations and the

Gnosis project. To his left, Captain Bradford was seated and across from him, Lieutenant Salina Gold, a scientist, sat with perfect posture.

The lead researcher, Doctor Lisa Harper, stood near the window, pacing nervously. Simon stepped back as Cassie entered and the door closed, leaving her alone with the others. She put on a smile and approached. "Hello, I'm Agent Cassandra Alexander of the AIA. I've been asked to attend this briefing and assist."

"We know," Admiral Reach replied. "I assume you know everyone in the room already since you spooks have files on the world, right?"

Cassie's cheeks flushed but she nodded. "Yes, I'm familiar with all your records and names."

"Good, then please have a seat and we'll get right down to business. We're dealing with an alien threat who came straight for the Orb. This concerns the entire world, especially since none of us here are naive enough to believe they won't be back for another shot later. My people are combing through the different bits of alien tech and we have a prisoner to interrogate."

"Sounds positive," Cassie said. "Has the … er … creature said anything? What's it look like?"

Doctor Harper tapped her tablet, bringing an image on a wall screen before answering. "We've performed a medical analysis and found him to be surprisingly similar to human beings. Same parts, same nourishment requirements and coloration. Some of their faculties seem to have developed differently but not significantly enough to matter."

"Such as?" Captain Bradford asked.

"They see better than us but their sense of smell is diminished." Doctor Harper shrugged. "Their tactile senses are also enhanced, perhaps to a hyper level where they might be able to feel vibrations and know what is causing it half a mile away. However, beyond those points, they are pretty much human beings."

"How does this even happen?" Admiral Reach asked. "What are the odds of such a similar species developing far from Earth?"

"Long before the Orb was discovered, we theorized about precursor races which may have seeded several planets. It didn't explain human evolution, however, which is a generally agreed upon point. Perhaps they influenced us all in subtle some way, nudging the development process, but we have no definitive proof of such a thing."

Doctor Harper continued, "in any event, our Orb is unlikely to be the only such device in the galaxy. Perhaps they put one on several habitable planets, waiting for the sentient races of those places to discover them. I'm speculating, of course. Wildly in fact."

"Of course," Admiral Reach muttered.

The implications of what Harper suggested made Cassie frown. She turned to the screen displaying the physiology of the enemy. The image could've been anyone she ever met. "So this is first contact. A species nearly indistinguishable from our own with different but not insurmountable technology. May I ask what the military proposes we do about it?"

Admiral Reach scowled. "These aliens have declared war on the human race. My inclination is to finish what they started. Determine where they came from, what they want and end their ability to make war."

Doctor Harper cleared her throat. "I'm not sure hostility is our best option, Admiral."

"They wouldn't even answer our hails," Captain Bradford said. "They came with the express intent of gaining access to the Orb and they planned on killing or destroying whatever got in their way. Something tells me that peace isn't exactly an option and believe me, I'd much rather pursue that than the alternative."

Lieutenant Gold held up her hand before speaking. "I believe we need to determine why they want the Orb. Depending on the answer to the question, we may know whether or not war is even necessary. For example, there's a possibility that this attack was one of desperation, something to save themselves from some kind of destruction."

"Meaning," Admiral Reach said, "that they might've brought everything they had for the effort."

"Nothing's impossible," Lieutenant Gold replied. "I wouldn't rule it out. Likewise, just because this particular faction did not feel like playing nice doesn't mean they represent their entire species. We may find there are more amiable individuals within their ranks. Diplomacy may still be an option."

Captain Bradford looked at Cassie. "What's the AIA assessment of this situation?"

"We're reserving any official opinion until the interrogation with the prisoner has been concluded." Cassie tried not to look like a deer caught in headlights. The question caught her off guard. "Has he been spoken to yet?"

Admiral Reach shook his head. "No, we performed the medical exam through his cell door and he has been in restraints since we took him prisoner. He hasn't uttered a sound as of yet and technicians are accessing the Orb for translation services. Assuming this thing can speak at all."

Doctor Harper glared at the Admiral. "I think we've established the prisoner as male. You can at least give the prisoner some dignity."

Captain Bradford hummed. "I'm pretty sure he or it doesn't care what we call it. Our notions of decency might be totally lost to these people. The best we can hope for is an explanation for what we're dealing with and why."

"I'd like to be in on the conversation," Cassie said. Her heart beat a little faster as she spoke, fear tickling her stomach. "I'm certain I can get something out of it … er … him. Would that be okay?"

"AIA has jurisdiction," Admiral Reach said. "At this point at least. When we determine whether or not we're dealing with a total monster or a bunch of potential war criminals … well, the military can take over from there."

"Understood." Cassie nodded, gesturing for the door. "Shall we start now? Something tells me we would like to get this underway as quickly as possible, especially if we're worried about a second attack."

"Indeed." Captain Bradford stood. "All things considered, the quicker he talks, the sooner we can plan our next move. Lead the way, Doctor Harper. I think we'd all like to see what this person has to say and whether or not we have to worry about a full-scale war breaking out between our people … and aliens from beyond our solar system."

☐

Chapter 3

Desmond had only met a few members of the AIA in his time. They tended to be much older than Cassie and not half as attractive. He found their choice of representatives surprising. They always seemed stuffy to him but even in her fancy white uniform, he sensed a defiant soul beneath. Someone that didn't necessarily adhere to the typical restrictions of her organization.

Perhaps they recognized that the situation they were in called for someone who thought outside the regimented box of rules and regulations. He was making assumptions, of course, and he knew judging the book by the cover never turned out well. How strict would she be about toeing the line?

I guess I'll find out soon enough.

They all went down to the security center where their holding cells were kept. The prisoner had been in one of the interrogation rooms for hours, enduring observation and hands-off medical examinations. No one had spoken with him yet but the guards stated he didn't respond when they handled him roughly.

Stepping up to the security glass, they peered in at their prisoner and the tension in the area rose noticeably. If the man sitting in that room were not wearing a uniform and had been identified as an alien, he would never have known the truth. Brown hair, pale skin, regular eyes … he could've been one of the Gnosis crew members.

"And we're sure he's not human?" Desmond asked. "That these people aren't some kind of separatist faction that just spent time away from the planet long enough to build up the appearance of an alien invasion?"

"As I said," Doctor Harper replied, "they may appear to be the same but there are differences. While we were unable to perform any invasive checks on this one, we did perform an autopsy on one of the dead ones … one which was mostly whole. This allowed us to confirm, without a shadow of a doubt, that they are not human."

Desmond nodded, thinking of the ramifications of the enemy's appearance. They could've been patient, infiltrated the planet and made their way here without the attack. Perhaps they felt a sense of urgency to get it done quickly. Maybe they were incapable of speech. Regardless, he dreaded the idea of a situation involving spies.

Admiral Reach drew a deep breath. "I was informed by command that my interrogator was to give the AIA representative first crack at the prisoner." He turned to Cassie. "Are you prepared?"

Desmond watched her closely and noted only a brief hesitation before she nodded. "I am."

"Are you armed?" Reach asked.

"No, sir. I only have my computer with me right now which I can use as a translation device." Cassie tapped the screen on the tablet. "Hopefully, we'll be able to find a common method of communicating."

"Very well. Go ahead. The guard will be with you with orders to react should anything strange happen."

"Understood." Cassie moved over to the door and nodded at the armed man waiting for her. He opened it up and they stepped inside. The alien didn't look up but Desmond detected a little tension increase in his face. Perhaps he was prepared to be hurt. The thought didn't bode well when considering what their culture might do to prisoners.

Desmond leaned close to Salina and whispered, "What's your take on all this? You've been pretty quiet."

"Considering what we're seeing with these aliens, I understand everyone's concerns. However, I'm worried about what this one might say if we can talk to him. Surrendering to the enemy is one thing but to creatures you know little about?" Salina shook her head. "He would have no idea what we might do to him or how badly this could go."

Desmond thought about the motivations of the alien. Survival might be too obvious but then again, reading too far into the situation might be just as dangerous. Either way, he bit his tongue and decided to simply watch the attempted interrogation. Could the young AIA officer get through to him?

Cassie put her tablet on the table, sat down and tapped a button. A beam of light shot from a sensor and ran over the alien's head. He flinched but didn't move. When it finished, she cleared her throat and began. "Hello. My name is Cassandra and I'd very much like to talk to you. This device has scanned you and will attempt to translate my words to your language."

A few moments passed before the device began to speak in what sounded like total gibberish. The syllables represented Japanese but none of it seemed familiar to Desmond. He looked at Salina who shrugged. It took a bit longer to repeat than when Cassie spoke it the first time but when it finished, she continued.

"You can speak plainly and the device will repeat your words in my language."

Again, the speaker pumped out more strange words. The alien looked up at her and smirked.

"We've studied your people and have a vague understanding of your … language." The translation device took a moment to translate the odd grunts and quick syllables. Having the words come out in a computerized monotone made them seem eerie and all the more alien. "Speak."

"I see," Cassie said. "Would you mind telling me your name then?"

"Revik," he replied.

"Why did you attack our planet, Revik?" Cassie asked. "What did you hope to accomplish? Were you after the Orb?"

"What you call the Orb, we refer to as Trindisha. They are powerful artifacts."

"Artifacts …" Cassie's eyes narrowed. "So you believe there are more of them. Does one exist on your planet as well?"

"Yes …" Revik chewed his lip. "There are many. They belonged to a race called the Trind. Have you not discovered this on your own? The histories should be present in every Trindisha."

"We haven't uncovered any histories," Cassie replied. "Why are you telling me all this?"

"If you are able to talk to me then my unit is dead and the attack vessels are all gone. I am alone here with no hope of rescue. They tasked us all to die before speaking but I could not obey." Revik looked away. "I dishonor everything about myself, my people and my family but I … I do not want to die."

"Coward then," Admiral Reach said. "Lucky for us, we got one that's so afraid of pain."

Desmond didn't buy it entirely. Perhaps the alien was scared and didn't want to be tortured but he didn't hold out at all. Did his race truly lack any discipline? He spoke of honor so they must've had some kind of code. Surrendering to avoid death seemed understandable but immediately talking? It felt like he might be offering up some misinformation.

"Do you think he's lying?" Desmond asked.

Doctor Harper checked her computer. "If he is, then the telltale signs of dishonesty don't apply to him."

"Tell me more about your people," Cassie asked. "What do you call yourselves?"

"We are Pahxin from well beyond your galaxy. Millions of light years away."

"Can you give us coordinates?" Cassie leaned forward and moved the tablet toward him. She tapped it a couple times and Desmond strained to see. She showed him star maps. "Where is your home in relation to ours?"

Very good. We can plan an assault that way if necessary.

"I …" Revik leaned to look at the screen. "You see … it would be …" He lifted his hand and let out a horrifying scream. Cassie very nearly fell out of her chair as she scrambled away from him. His hands slapped his forehead as the guard raised his weapon and aimed it at him. Doctor Harper opened the door and rushed in.

"Don't shoot!" She cried. "Something's happening in his head!"

Salina joined her, using her own scanner before backing away. She glanced back at Desmond and shook her head. He frowned, motioning for her to come back. Before the science officer made it to the door, blood began flowing freely from Revik's nose and he began twitching violently.

Doctor Harper pressed a device to the side of his head and tapped a button several times but nothing seemed to happen. A moment later, the screaming stopped and Revik slumped in his seat unmoving. Salina moved over and whispered in Desmond's ear, letting him know Revik must've died.

"How?" Desmond asked.

"Some kind of brain hemorrhage." Salina looked at her tablet. "It came on suddenly when he reached out for the device."

"A trigger?" Admiral Reach asked. "Some kind of method to protect their home in the event of capture."

"Seems like it." Desmond rubbed his forehead and stepped into the cell. He joined Cassie and touched her shoulder, making her jump. "Are you okay?"

Cassie nodded quickly, composing herself. She reached for her tablet but stopped. Blood splattered the surface, small drops and a larger glob near the bottom. Desmond picked it up and wiped it clean with his sleeve before offering it to her. She didn't seem like she wanted to take it but did anyway, swallowing hard.

"He's dead," Doctor Harper announced. "So sudden!"

"When he tried to tell me where he was from," Cassie said. "They must've conditioned these people. I bet there were other topics that could've done the same thing. Far more effective than trusting them to kill themselves, they simply have to be killed by their interrogators. That … was devilishly clever … and horrifying."

"We understand a lot though," Desmond said. "Real revelations. There are more Orbs out there and aliens as well."

"And people who will kill for them," Admiral Reach added. "But as much as these things are intriguing, we don't know what to do next."

"Their computers." Cassie looked at Admiral Reach. "I need access to their devices. Any that are intact. I should be able to gather data from them and perhaps figure out where they were going next … or something like that. They seemed to be trying to collect more Orbs. We need to figure out why."

"I don't care about why," Admiral Reach said. "I just want to know where they are so we can kill them."

Doctor Harper scowled at him. "Motivations are necessary to start a war, don't you think?"

Admiral Reach looked her in the eyes, ticking off points. "They attacked our fleet, assaulted your facility and killed our people. Do you think the dead soldiers and researchers care much about what motivated them to do so? And do you believe the human race wants to find a peaceful solution with our attackers?"

"Has the human race been informed of exactly what happened?" Harper asked. Desmond exchanged a knowing look with Salina. The media outlets discussed the orbital conflict. They didn't say anything about the assault on Gamma Alpha, not yet. Now that they knew why they were attacked, but it would likely come up.

The truth might unify people behind a serious war effort, even if it took humanity well beyond their solar system. Never mind the fact they would need to build additional ships to wage any real campaign and the training to go with them. If Admiral Reach wasn't nervous about the prospect of combat, he should've been.

Earth had the resources and utilized new technology every month. At least they'd be ready quickly providing the enemy didn't come in greater numbers before they could prepare. The possibility made Desmond twitchy. While Revik made it sound like they were only there for an orb, they very well could've been an expeditionary force, paving the way for an invasion.

"We'll handle the PR part of this, Doctor," Admiral Reach said. "You worry about the research part. Help that young lady with her investigation into the technology and report back to us as soon as possible. In fact, how long do you feel you'll need before you can tell us something?"

"It depends on what it takes for us to decrypt it," Harper said. "At least a day. Possibly two."

"Alright, as long as we have something soon." Admiral Reach turned away and started down the hall.

"We don't have much more time as I'm sure you're well aware. Captain Bradford, please join me in the conference room. We've got a few things to discuss before you go back to your regular duties."

"Yes, sir." Desmond nodded. He turned to Salina. "Stick around and see if you can help out at all. It's a rare opportunity to work with the Orb, right?"

"Of course, sir. Thank you." Salina smiled, which was a rare expression for the serious woman. "I'll see you later then."

"Good luck." Desmond turned and hurried after the Admiral. *I hope we don't need it.*

***

Cassie had never seen someone die in her presence. The horror on the man's face combined with his screaming shocked her but she couldn't let it get to her. Still, even years of training didn't prepare her for what she experienced in the interrogation room. It had been going so well before the incident. In the back of her mind, she knew something wasn't right.

He shouldn't have been so quick to tell me what he did. Maybe he also realized we'd get a lot of the data from their computer devices. However, now that we know their people are sabotaged, we have to be careful with the gear too. If they had no qualms about sacrificing a life, they'd likely do the same to a computer.

Harper brought her to one of the analytics rooms where they'd be able to observe and study the various devices confiscated from the bodies. Lieutenant Salina Gold accompanied them which made some sense. As the head science officer aboard the Gnosis, she would have the best chance of helping them from the military side of the house.

Admiral Reach would definitely appreciate her involvement.

Computer banks lined the walls with several terminals for people to interface with. Three tables occupied the center of the room, their smooth metal surfaces littered with the bits of alien technology they were able to salvage. Some seemed intact while others were trashed from the skirmish.

Armor sat on one of the tables, light weight and only covering the torso. It struck Cassie as odd until she noticed the box on the front which had lenses on the sides. A quick scan indicated they produced a personal shield capable of taking several direct shots and probably an unlimited number of grazes.

"What do you think?" Cassie asked. "Do they power these with some kind of battery or something else entirely?"

Salina stepped forward. "It would make sense if they did a renewable energy source, something allowing them to recycle the power continuously. Otherwise, they would burn out long before they finished a fight."

Doctor Harper sat at one of the terminals and began typing. "I've captured the video data we have from the conflict. The shields were able to take our normal small-arms fire and shrug off the damage but they didn't have such an easy time with the power armor weapons. Those packed a much harder punch and tore through the defenses quite easily."

"That's to be expected," Cassie said. "They were only prepared for our standard defenses. Note that they waited to attack until the Gnosis was on its maiden voyage, far enough from Earth to give them a chance. If our fleet hadn't been able to hold them off … If your people hadn't been so amazing, then this situation may not have ended favorably."

Salina tapped the table. "Before we do any further analysis, may I suggest we isolate the items we're interested in to ensure they don't self-destruct like the prisoner did? If these short out or worse, explode, the damage could be substantially worse than what happened in the interrogation room."

"My thoughts exactly," Cassie said. "Can you initiate the containment fields on the tables, Doctor?"

"I'm on it now." Harper tapped a few keys and a blue, transparent dome burst over each table. The energy hummed and crackled as it stabilized. "Let's start with some surface scans to determine if there are any incendiary devices that might be dangerous."

"Will you be able to disarm them?" Salina asked.

Cassie hummed. "It depends on how they armed the devices I suppose. The good news is the containment field is powerful enough to handle some pretty serious detonations. Right, Doctor?"

Harper chuckled. "You don't sound entirely sure, Cassie. But yes, we've tested it extensively and I can say with certainty we can handle whatever they might put against us. I've also isolated each individual item within their own field so that if one goes, it won't take them all. The energy field provides the scanning so we're ready to begin."

Cassie nodded. "I'll take the computers if you don't mind."

"I'm on the armor," Harper replied. "Lieutenant Gold, you're on the weapons. Report back in ten minutes."

Cassie wirelessly connected her own device to the terminal, gaining access to the dozens of applications she'd specifically updated with what she learned from studying the Orb's coding structure. As these creatures likely built their technology with their own version, she hoped it might grant her an advantage in cracking it.

The initial scans showed no incendiary devices nor any obvious form of sabotage. The next step, a tentative probe, didn't reveal anything. Cassie needed to power it up for any further testing and it seemed possible to do so remotely. Her hand started to sweat just a moment before she hit the button which would initiate the startup sequence.

The alien computer clicked on, the screen lighting up green for a moment before displaying a high resolution image of a diamond shape. It took less than five seconds to boot up and she initiated a translation app. Her heart skipped a beat when the message came back that there was a code match.

It's not exact but I'll be able to extrapolate from here. Once I get a few more similarities, we can build a codex and teach the application how to talk to this thing. Then we'll get to the heart of their data and whether or not they stored anything useful on these devices.

Once the device came online, it sent out a burst of data. A quick scan showed it was attempting to wirelessly connect with something in orbit as well as the other computers on the table. The individual forcefields kept the signal local but she noted the activity. She'd want to turn off the signal as soon as she took control.

Patience was the name of the game and Cassie had to take a couple deep breaths to avoid tapping her foot. The others around her worked with severe intensity, staring at their screens as if they might will the computers to work faster. They had time to get their work done so Cassie forced herself to relax, letting her shoulders slump and the muscles in her back loosen.

The root directory of the device came online but Cassie didn't simply want to navigate through their interface. She wanted direct access to the database beneath. That would allow her to run her own queries and gather the data much faster. If the alien's method of storing data was roughly the same as humanity's, she'd have several ready-made scripts for the task.

"We're at the ten minute mark," Doctor Harper said. "Do you have anything to report?"

Salina started, "The weapons are not sabotaged. I suspect any sort of device they would've installed may have been too unstable to ensure it would not go off during an inopportune combat moment. They carried two types of firearm, energy and something else. The former I'm still analyzing, including the power cores, and the latter … I haven't figured out."

"What do you mean?" Harper asked. "What's so odd about them?"

"They appear to have exhausted all the ammunition in them. I'm not getting any energy readings though they are, at the very least, electric. I suspect they fire projectiles and they simply exhausted them all but I have to reverse engineer them, at least through simulation, to know for sure. I'll have another update in an hour or so."

"Perfect." Harper paused a moment before asking, "how're the computers coming?"

Cassie gave her a quick update on where she was at. She turned in her chair. "My applications are on it but they'll need some time. I don't know if an hour will cut it but I think that's a fair regroup time. Where are you at, Doctor?"

Harper took a deep breath before answering. "Well ... these folks used power in a very efficient manner. Before today, I would've said we were incredible when it came to how we managed energy. These personal shields are a great example of how we practically had no idea what we were doing."

"What do you mean?" Salina said. "How do they work?"

"They attach them to the armor, which has a network of power lines all throughout the plates. These connect up at the shield itself, which allows the shield to emit from the four lenses. What we failed to notice was there were receivers on the back to relay the power and ensure consistent defense all around the body.

"However, there are two weak points: the head and the lower legs. The chest and back are heavily protected and could take the most punishment. The shield itself does not get covered but it is the thickest part of the armor. My analysis shows it could take at least two to three direct hits ... and it's a pretty small target anyway."

Cassie frowned. "Incredible technology. How's the power efficiency so great?"

"An initial charge turns the unit on," Harper replied. "The body itself acts as a generator of sorts. When they are breathing, they're generating more power. The material surrounding the armor is also porous and tiny follicles are able to collect ambient radiation. An inhale-exhale motion moves the energy and keeps the shields working."

Salina asked, "So if someone held their breath the process would stop?"

"No, a standard charge would last for fifteen minutes without any motion at all." Harper shrugged. "Indefinitely, if the person breathes normally."

"What else do you have to figure out?" Cassie joked. "You seem to have got the whole thing down."

"I still don't know what material they used for any of this," Harper replied. "Nor have I been able to break down what they used for the projector lenses. I have only hit our local database. I'll have to hit the Orb to get more data on that part I think. And the power relays … We wouldn't have done it this way so I've got some study to do there, too."

"What about the ships?" Salina asked. "Surely, we must have the debris coming back soon. How's the salvage operation going?"

"Slowly," Harper said. "Only one of the enemy vessels remained remotely intact but that isn't saying much. The initial assessment shows even that ship lost the power core when it exploded. We might get something from individual systems but the crews are calling their find a total loss. Still, they're bringing back what they've got. I expect them by tomorrow morning."

Cassie's computer beeped and pulled her attention back to the screen. "I'm back on," she said. "We'll talk again in an hour. Hey ... can we have someone bring us some water or something? If we're going to live down here, I'm parched."

Harper nodded. "I'm on it."

The code matching software found all similarities and began to create a translation for those parts it didn't understand. Cassie tapped into the Orb to give her program a larger dictionary to work from. The work looked like it wouldn't take too long. Despite the events that brought about this situation, she couldn't help but be excited.

This find proved so many theories she and her colleagues discussed back at the AIA. They knew aliens existed elsewhere in the galaxy, at least at some point in history. The Orb itself, with its ordered data structure and vast storage archives, proved some kind of intelligent creature built it.

The debates ranged from precursor spacefaring cultures to gods. One of her older colleagues presented a paper on how the Greeks may have had access to the Orb and used that assumption to explain away their old pantheon. Even after years of study, humanity only scratched the surface of what the ancient device could do.

However, Cassie found it hard to believe a Greek named Zeus discovered the Orb and learned how to shape shift, throw lightning bolts and guide the future of mankind. If they accepted such a thing, then all historical fictions had to come into question. Was there truly a hero like Beowulf who fought a great monster or was that a nonfiction account of the Orb meddling in human affairs?

The theories sounded romantic but Cassie had to dismiss them. She founded her opinions on logic and possibility. Considering how they had to access the Orb, how they needed computer interfaces to interpret the data, she couldn't imagine early man working with it at all other than to perhaps worship it.

Of course, if the theory about a culture meddling in the development of planets across the galaxy turned out to be true, then perhaps it was possible for early man to access it. Atlantis came up several times in debate. An ancient nation capable of wonders. If they discovered a method to interface the device, then maybe all the rumors about them were true.

But why did they vanish? And how had humanity never uncovered their splendors?

Cassie didn't like going down the path to answer those questions, not earnestly. The answers generally were apocalyptic in nature and too frightening to indulge. Much as she liked to take things to logical conclusions, this was one time she didn't feel it necessary. Especially when she was about to pop the directory structure on the computer.

Focus your mind on the here and now. It's safer … and a lot less depressing.

***

Desmond sat through a briefing with Admiral Reach concerning the next steps. The situation took only a few minutes because they didn't have a lot to go on. They needed to wait for the findings of their research team to give some clear direction for a path forward. In the meantime, the Gnosis was to repair and prepare for … something.

"You have operational authority over the research and planning," Reach said. "I'm sure you understand how curious your crew is right now so decide how much you intend to tell them. Considering how huge this situation is, I have a feeling they'll want something more than vague notions. Having a front row seat to an alien invasion will have an impact on those who were there."

"I thought about it," Desmond said. "I'll work with our section chiefs and ensure we have this under control."

"Good." Reach stood. "I have to report to high command and let them know what's going on. When you have information, interrupt whatever I'm doing. My aide will know to do so. The council isn't going to be thrilled at how little info I have right now so anything I can throw their way will help me out."

"Understood." Desmond got up as well. "Good luck, sir."

"Thank you, Captain. To you as well."

After Reach left, Desmond contacted Vincent. The commander answered by shouting over quite a ruckus behind him. "Commander Bowman here!"

"What's going on up there, Vincent?" Desmond asked. "What's all the noise?"

"I'm down in engineering! Give me a moment." The loud noise became quieter. "I've stepped out of the room. During repairs of the minor systems, they discovered a vulnerability and are taking steps to make it safer. Apparently, one of the generators wasn't very well protected and if it would've exploded, people could've gotten hurt."

"I'm glad they caught it." Desmond hummed, wondering what other issues they needed to address. "We have research teams studying the various tech and bodies of the aliens. Admiral Reach put me in charge so I'm going to run operations from the office here. Are you okay to continue command in my absence?"

"Yes, sir. I'm just lending a hand where I can right now and checking in on everyone."

"Good. I'll keep you informed of what's going on as it comes up. For now, ensure we're ready for another long voyage. How's the pilot who got shot down?"

"A few bumps and bruises only. The medics have already released him to quarters for some bed rest." Vincent paused a moment, muttering to a person on the other end of the com. "Sorry about that. He'll be ready for our next engagement in a day or two."

"Perfect. Check in with the rest of the fleet as well and see where they're at. I'm assuming they've got search and rescue still out there. I want a full report on all the people we've found and … and the ones we've lost too." Desmond sat back down. "Then get me a defensive analysis. How ready are we for another attack?"

"I'm on it, sir."

"Thank you. I'll catch up with you later. Desmond out." The captain turned to his computer and stared at the screen, thoughtful for several long minutes. He didn't have a specific direction to take at the moment but needed to allow people to get their jobs done without him badgering them for results.

Casualty reports came in both from the Gnosis and the rest of the fleet. His stomach felt heavy as he went through the long list of names from those who were lost in the initial attack. They fought valiantly to hold the enemy off long enough to get the support they needed. They may have been able to defeat the attack but what would the cost have been?

Desmond knew the man who had to deliver the tragic news to the parents of the fallen for the other ships in the fleet. He didn't envy him the task and quietly thanked God he didn't have to do the same. The relief would be short lived if they truly went to war and a peaceful resolution seemed beyond unlikely.

If the enemy came with a mere expeditionary force, they may have only sent lighter vessels too. Larger capital ships held the potential to be truly devastating. With the Gnosis as the most advanced ship, they really needed additional versions to hold back a real tide of any appreciable magnitude.

How fast can we build more ships? I know they were taking their time with a more combat focused version of the Gnosis. That project has been fast tracked, I guarantee it. Will this be like America in World War Two? Will they dedicate every factory and available-to-hand to bolster our military?

Once they released some version of the truth to the public about the attack, they'd have the necessary support to do so. Fear and patriotism would drive people to support an effort to defend the entire race against whatever lurked out there beyond the borders of the solar system. Prior to the attack, they had planned to discover wonders.

Unfortunately, wonders came looking for them and they didn't want to play nice.

☐

Chapter 4

Four Days Later

Cassie never slept at Gamma Alpha before and was surprised the quarters were so comfortable. The first day they dove into studying the various alien pieces of equipment saw her working well into the night. Despite the fact she found so many similarities in the code, the information itself proved to be encrypted and worse, requiring translation.

All the next day and most of the night, she applied dozens of ciphers and even created several new ones. Sleeping proved difficult with the frustration despite exhaustion clinging to her. On the third day, others tried to offer some advice but she'd gone down such an advanced track, they didn't have anything new to offer.

However, after more coffee than she cared to admit and a walk outside, she made a breakthrough. One of her ciphers, possibly the most basic of them, worked. Combined with the translation software from the Orb, the epiphany allowed her to break through their encryption. When her application finished running, she had full access to the data stored on the device.

No one was around to share the triumph but she clapped anyway. Punch drunk from all the caffeine and too little sleep, she backed the data up to a separate hard drive and started running her queries. The Orb translated the words on the fly, giving her a remarkably legible set of text files.

The videos would require more time to decode but they had plenty of them. Based on the directory structure and what the Orb converted the text to say, she guessed they might be video journals of whoever carried the device. They might be insightful into the purpose of the attack. When she found their orders, she knew she had hit the jackpot.

After four days of working on it, Cassie had to present her findings in the evening after dinner. Someone brought her stuff from her apartment so she didn't have to wear the stupid uniform anymore, opting instead for a pair of comfortable slacks and a blouse. When she showed up to the conference room, the audience was somewhat smaller than she anticipated.

Captain Bradford, Admiral Reach, Doctor Harper and Lieutenant Gold were all present. A scribe sat at the back of the room, a young technician with a tablet ready to take notes. She closed the door behind her and took a seat quietly, waiting for the meeting to begin. Everyone was staring at their computers until the Admiral spoke up.

"Alright, we've come together for a discovery meeting. What've you learned and how much more time do you need?"

Doctor Harper started, "We've performed investigations into the equipment of the aliens and their bodies. At the physiological level, they are no different than we are and by that I mean they can't take any more punishment. They're sturdy creatures, capable of adapting to several environments. Our atmosphere would not have been harmful to them however …

"They were not prepared for some of the germs we've developed here. As I did my investigation it was pretty clear that they'd suffer from some of our more advanced illnesses. The healthiest of them might've lived through such a thing but one in poor shape would have had a problem."

"So they could die from a cold?" Desmond asked. "Like in War of the Worlds?"

"It's a distinct possibility," Harper said, "however, I can tell you we did find an as of yet unidentified substance in their bodies. Our chemists don't know what it's for. I'm guessing they have developed a universal inoculation though. It would make sense for a space faring people who had been exploring for a while."

"I trust you are borrowing this idea?" Admiral Reach asked.

"We're attempting to figure out how they anticipated what the body needed," Harper replied. "They may simply be boosting the immune system but with all of them dead, it's harder to tell. Couple that with the fact the substance we discovered is made up of ingredients we've never seen. We'll get it soon, however."

"Good work." Admiral Reach turned to his tablet. "Anything else on that front?"

"The more technical data has been sent to all of your accounts," Harper said. "You can find their autopsy reports and physical details there. If you have any questions, please don't hesitate to ask me."

"Lieutenant Gold." Admiral Reach gestured to the science officer. "What're you presenting?"

"Weapons and armor, sir." Lieutenant Gold stood up and moved over to the large TV. She brought up a number of videos and let them play in the four different corners. "Doctor Harper helped with the initial plunge into their defenses but I took over the next morning. We were able to actually use some of their equipment and tested it all."

One of the videos showed a fully armored soldier taking a shot with one of the alien pistols in the firing range. The beam cut through the target, incinerating it. Another depicted their armor, fully repaired, taking several projectile shots and coming out unscathed. She also showed off their personal shields and how they reacted with their own weapons.

"As you can see, their own beam weapons cannot pierce their personal shields. Ours are on a different frequency and are therefore able to penetrate their defenses. I'm of the impression they had enough foresight to pump up their offensive and defensive capabilities but they didn't seem to have enough data to fully negate our attacks."

"What've you been able to do about measuring their effectiveness?" Admiral Reach asked. "Do you know how we can bolster our defenses to the same potency?"

"To some extent, yes," Lieutenant Gold replied. "Our power armor already proved to be effective and the Gnosis can take some of the punishment of their larger weapons. The bubble weapon … that one concerns us though." She brought up a video of the incident. "We were unable to recover what did that but Agent Alexander may be able to fill in some blanks."

"Do we even know what that was?" Desmond gestured to the screen. "It wiped out shields fast but didn't even touch theirs."

"Another frequency issue." Lieutenant Gold shrugged. "My own scans showed they rapidly cycled through various fields and somehow, that bubble still didn't damage them. Schematics would be nice but for now, we simply have to be ready for them to do it. I've marked exactly what it looked like on the scanner moments before they let it loose."

Admiral Reach nodded. "You've uploaded this to the fleet?"

"Yes, sir." Lieutenant Gold tapped the side of the monitor. "At the orders I received from high command, I disseminated these videos to all military commanders. They have them to research and study."

"Excellent." Reach narrowed his eyes. "What're the chances of us surviving another exchange with these creatures?"

"I'm merely speculating based on my research," Lieutenant Gold replied. "And my first field of study is not military tactics. However, considering their technology and what we've learned alone, I'd say we've increased our survivability exponentially. We understand so much more now, we can defend against it. Providing we work on counters soon."

Desmond checked his tablet and noted she'd sent a lengthy report. "Are those recommendations in this file?"

"Among many other things, sir. The technical details are all fully laid out and prepared for the engineers to assist with implementation."

"Good." Admiral Reach turned to Cassie. "Agent Alexander, are you ready to present your own information?"

"I am." Cassie paced by Lieutenant Gold and accessed the screen with her tablet. She brought up an image of one of the people. "First off, we know they call their race the Pahxin from our interrogation. The ones who attacked us are a faction within that race, the Tol'An. They seem to be some kind of fanatical group."

"What're they fanatical about?" Admiral Reach asked.

"Technology. Collecting it, at least." Cassie shrugged. "Their exact mission statement was not available for study and I'm inferring their obsession based on the notes they've taken on the Orb." She put an image of the Orb up. "This came from one of the enemy devices. They had it in their mission briefing and it was amidst a set of messages all marked as high priority. Each member of the alien crew were required to study this."

"The Orb?" Admiral Reach frowned. "We knew they were after the Orb, Agent. What's the point?"

"This ... is not our Orb." Cassie's message made them all fall silent. Even the scribe looked up. "Those of us who have studied the device extensively always suspected there were others. The AIA itself investigated alien life but we couldn't draw any concrete conclusions, not even with full access to the device.

"However, the alien tech proves out that our Orb is one of many and this race of creatures, these aliens, are attempting to bring them all together."

"For what purpose?" Desmond asked. "Why are they doing it?"

"These were soldiers," Cassie replied. "The why wasn't listed. They were told to collect the Orb at all cost. Furthermore, they've been lingering around our solar system for several weeks planning this assault.

They knew precisely when the Gnosis was to leave and gave you plenty of time to get well away from the planet before attacking."

"We suspected that ..." Desmond sighed. "I guess confirmation is nice. So what else did you pull from it?"

"The more specific details and personal information from different alien creatures are in my report," Cassie said. "Their commanders believed this would be an easy extraction. Their initial attack force was twice the size of what we faced. However, when the Gnosis left, they split so they might save some time."

Admiral Reach's brows lifted. "Doing what?"

"Going after another one." Cassie brought up a star chart on the screen. "Here. Thirteen solar systems away from our current location. The rest of their force went to a planet all the way out there to gather another Orb. You see, I've now confirmed the race responsible for these devices was spread across the cosmos."

Desmond squinted at the screen. "You think they left one of these on every planet they seeded, right?"

"Yes, I think they're responsible for sentient life spreading throughout the galaxy," Cassie replied. "And they eventually wanted us to find the Orb and take to the stars ourselves. Maybe join them ... but I'm of the impression something happened. They're gone and now their children are rushing to find the answers to where they came from."

"And punch their brothers in the face while doing so," Admiral Reach muttered. "Fascinating discoveries, Agent. You have the coordinates for this other planet?"

"They're in the report," Cassie replied. "Our hyperspace drives could make the trip in ten hours. The aliens have had a four day head start but I can tell you this. Their smaller ships weren't as efficient with faster than light travel. If you intend to stop them … if you want to intervene, we will very likely catch them unawares while they attempt to extract that new Orb."

"Or while they're in the middle of a massive battle," Desmond said. "After all, the planet they're going after might be just like ours. Inhabited with people who aren't ready to just hand over their stuff."

Admiral Reach nodded. "Yes, I expect as much." He stood. "I am taking all of your notes to the council and will discuss our next steps. It looks like we need to make some fast decisions. Desmond, I recommend you take Lieutenant Gold and Agent Alexander back to the Gnosis right away. I'll contact you there with our decision."

"Yes, sir." Desmond stood and offered a salute as the flag officer left the room. He turned away from the door. "Grab your things. We'll be wheels up in thirty minutes."

Cassie watched him leave, her heart racing in her chest. After four days of study, things seemed to really move into high gear. Leaving the planet at short notice made her nervous but she understood the urgency. Once the military knew what they were up against and what their enemies were doing, they were going to try to stop them.

After presenting them a valid reason to go after the aliens, Cassie knew in the back of her head they'd be heading out soon. There was still a chance the high council would recommend they hold off and not risk their ships on the errand. However, the Admiral seemed persuasive in his way and she expected that after a short debate, they'd relent.

The amount of pushback they provided would all depend on how close they were to finishing their new military ship. Those vessels damaged in the initial fight had been restored to fighting condition. Reports suggested they had some time left to finish all repairs, they could perform them while patrolling the system.

Some of the engineers at Gamma Alpha worked up plans to retrofit them with better defenses and some heavier offensive capabilities. Now that data existed to compare against, they knew how to give the rest of the fleet more of an edge in combat. The challenge came down to whether they could do it in time.

Doctor Harper helped put a schedule together so they wouldn't have to take more than a couple ships down at a time for updates. Shuttles were being packed with different types of equipment, supplies to upgrade shields and weapon systems. Calibration of the technology would be a solid start but in some cases, sturdier components were needed to withstand the extra energy output.

Performing such upgrades, or at least helping to ensure they were performing the proper upgrades would've been a job for Cassie had she not been drafted to help the Gnosis with their potential mission. The thought of leaving the solar system never crossed her mind. She'd been an analyst for so long, field work started to look like it wouldn't happen.

Now I get the chance to put some of these skills to use.

Lieutenant Gold patted her shoulder on the way out. "I'll see you on the shuttle, Agent."

"Um … you too." Cassie replied. Hurrying back to her quarters, she grabbed the three bags she packed the night before and took a brisk walk toward the landing field. A tiny part of her brain screamed at her about how she might never see Earth again if she boarded the ship. Going into war, being a crew member on a battleship, might be the last thing she ever did.

They can use me. I know it. I've got the experience and knowledge to help.

They'd need to study the ship schematics they took from the alien computers. Cassie had them all stored on her computer and assumed Captain Bradford would as well. Once they were aboard, she would send him a meeting invitation to go over the weaknesses and strengths of the opposition.

Cassie stepped outside into a warm breeze. Soldiers and technicians dashed about and massive transports moved heavy equipment to various parts of the structure. She'd been to Gamma Alpha several times but never seen it bustling in such a manner. The controlled chaos made her head spin.

Technicians installed new weapons at the hard points around the base and enhanced anti-aircraft cannons occupied the hills to either side of the structure. An energy field would be installed soon, something to provide some protection against a crashing vessel or projectiles. Each new addition made Gamma Alpha that much safer.

The shield technology existed before but with a little help and determination, engineers found a way to make the energy consumption far more efficient. These new deflectors could be raised as soon as enemies were detected closing in on Earth. Eventually, a method to keep them on at all times would be discovered.

Maybe major cities need the same treatment. It's a miracle the attackers only hit this place. Had they gone after a couple of large population centers, our military may have been too distracted to stop them from achieving their goals.

The question became whether they chose not to do so because they were civilized, didn't think of it or simply didn't have the manpower to pull it off. The basics of their plan were laid out in the computer: distract the military in orbit, hit the facility hard with ground troops and claim the Orb for their own.

Nothing in the orders suggested they had a contingency plan if they couldn't break through the defenses. They committed everything to the attack. While the aliens lingered in the solar system studying humanity, they may have discovered that Earth didn't know there were other creatures in the universe.

The invasion itself may have been enough of a surprise for them to risk everything.

Cassie arrived at the shuttle at the same time as the others. The whine of the turbine made it impossible to hear but Desmond gestured for them to board ahead of him. He followed, slapping a button on the wall to close the door. The moment it sealed, they were plunged into near silence. Alerts from the cockpit computers were the only sounds.

"We'll be at the Gnosis in fifteen minutes," Desmond said. "Stow your things and we'll get moving right away."

Cassie stuffed her bags into a storage bin at the back and took a seat, strapping in. The shuttle she took from her home in Geneva to Gamma Alpha was far more comfortable, with civilian luxuries the military vessel didn't bother with. Her seat lacked padding, just cold metal and the walls were utilitarian without panels to hide the infrastructure beneath.

The Gnosis isn't like this. These smaller ships must've been cheaper this way.

Because people were expected to live on the Gnosis, the engineers made it as comfortable as possible. One of the larger expenses came from the way they gave it some personality, just shy of an ancient luxury liner from the nineteen hundreds. The recreation areas had burgundy carpets and warm toned fabric panels on the walls.

The more technical areas erred on the side of high tech with metal floors and no-nonsense brown cushioned seats. But their quarters were designed to give people a chance to unwind in a pleasant way. Psychologists helped to design some of the finer points of the ship after several studies suggested prolonged space travel might be mentally unbalancing.

Defense ships tended to stay in orbit for short periods of time, essentially going on patrol for a few days at a time before rotating out their crews. It allowed people to be on planet enough to shake off any deleterious side effects of space travel but it didn't give researchers much to go on concerning their mental state.

Now I get the opportunity to help prove it for them with this next trip.

The ship launched, lifting slowly upward before tilting toward the sky. Cassie gripped her safety straps, drawing a deep breath just before the thrusters kicked in. They were hurtled away from the surface, the ship rattling wildly as they went. She did her best to remain cool, especially since Desmond and Salina didn't seem to even notice.

The turbulence became far worse the higher they went until the straps dug into her shoulders and made her head ache. Suddenly, it all stopped and the ship became silent and still. The inertial dampeners kicked in as they broke orbit, promising a smooth ride the rest of the way. Cassie forced herself to relax, tension slowly lifting from her muscles.

"First time in orbit?" Salina asked.

"No," Cassie replied. "But it is the first time I've had to get here so quickly. Civilian ships tend to take a little more time. They gradually ascend."

Desmond nodded. "Yeah, they're more cautious. Anyway, we haven't had time to really get to know each other much it's been so busy. Plus, your file's a little light. You probably know everything there is to know about us but … maybe you can share some details about yourself."

Cassie's cheeks burned. "I've seen the crew files for the Gnosis but I didn't pour over them in great detail. Um … so … I'm originally from California but moved to Geneva to attend the Advanced Technical Academy. The

AIA recruited me just before I graduated and I've been working with them ever since."

"How'd your parents feel about that assignment?" Desmond asked.

Cassie looked away. "I'm afraid they … well, they died before I graduated. I'd like to think they would be happy for me but dad tended to be a conspiracy theorist. He probably would've had some strong opinions about my employers and what they were up to."

Desmond smiled, though she saw more sadness than anything in his eyes. "I'm sorry to hear that. My dad was the same way, actually. Always looking in the shadows for a story other people didn't want him to hear." He sighed and shook his head. "Anyway, I grew up in Florida and Salina there is the most uptight Oregonian you'll ever meet."

"Always appreciate the praise, Captain." Salina smirked. "You'll find a fairly diverse group on the Gnosis from all corners of the Earth. Our bridge crew is mostly American with the exception of Deacon Neville, who is one of our pilots. He's from London originally."

"I'd like to offer—" Desmond interrupted himself as his computer began to ding. He placed something in his ear and turned away. "Go ahead, sir." A pause. "What? Are you … serious? That fast?" He nodded slowly. "I see. We're not quite aboard but will be there shortly. I'll contact you once we're there."

"What's going on?" Salina asked.

"Admiral Reach spoke to the council and they've already agreed that we need to get out there." Desmond seemed shocked. "He made quite the point about the head start the aliens had and how we needed to get moving."

Cassie narrowed her eyes. "What're the orders?"

"We're to find out why they want the Orb," Desmond replied. "And stop them from getting this one. Whatever information we can dig up. If, for some reason, the new Orb is not protected, they want us to bring it back to Gamma Alpha."

"What about defense here?" Salina looked at Cassie. "We all know that we're in a situation that's pretty tenuous with that."

Desmond shook his head. "They're close on the sister ship to the Gnosis, the one that's more military leaning. The rest of the fleet is repaired and they're upgrading them as we speak. But, the council doesn't believe the aliens are going to attack again soon. After all, they haven't had a chance to find out they failed yet."

"And it could take time," Cassie added. "After all, even if they were expecting a communication transmission, it wouldn't have arrived yet. Our best bet is to use the hyperspace drive and get there as soon as possible."

"We'll need some precise coordinates," Salina said.

"We have them." Cassie grinned, tapping her computer. "We took them from the aliens along with a star chart of the destination. We'll be able to hop in and take a look with long range scanners before diving into a full-on battle. And considering that I calculated a ten hour trip, we'll be able to examine the schematics for their ships, giving us a tactical advantage."

"At least the ones they left at Earth," Desmond said. "Okay, so we have clearance to depart as soon as we're ready. I'll contact Vincent and let him know we're mission active. I expect we'll be leaving the solar system in less than an hour." He paused. "Can't decide how I feel about it."

"A rational emotion would be fear," Salina pointed out. "Though I expect no one on board's normal enough for that."

Desmond chuckled. "No, we've all been itching to get moving. Unfortunately, our first trip involves combat. Still, we can't complain too much. After all, this is the opportunity of a lifetime, right?"

"Definitely," Cassie said. "One of the most historic events for humanity since we first set foot on the moon … since the discovery of the Orb even. Pressing beyond what so many people thought was a prison. We've conquered distance and now, we have the chance to see what's out there. For good or ill, we're the pioneers of our species."

Salina hummed. "So no pressure at all then, right?"

"None at all." Desmond motioned with his head toward the cockpit. "We're about to dock with the ship. Get ready. When we disembark, we're going to be busy for a while."

***

Vincent waited in the hangar bay for the Captain's shuttle to land. He'd received word before they left to expect an AIA agent who was joining the crew and to have the ship ready for immediate departure. They did everything they could without the coordinates for their destination and all on-duty personnel were at their stations.

Fighters were lined up, prepared to launch. They had enough backup vessels to replace the one they lost in the initial fight. Lieutenant Hal Brown had sufficiently recovered to return to his duties and already had a session with a psychologist to ensure he was mentally prepared. After being cleared for active duty, he returned to his unit.

The marines had now had a couple of days of downtime and were itching for another shot at the enemy. Their eagerness didn't sit well with Vincent but he understood the necessity of such warriors in the military. If everything had gone according to plan, those men would've been terribly bored with the original plan.

We're putting them to the test now. I should be grateful they're here.

Vincent always looked forward to space travel and visiting other star systems. He was an explorer at heart, always curious about what was beyond the horizon. The Gnosis assignment had been his dream come true and when they got the distress call from Earth, his heart sank.

He'd studied tactics in the academy. He knew how to conduct an offensive but the idea of actively serving in a war hadn't really occurred to him. After so many years of relative peace, with only minor skirmishes springing up here and there, he thought conflict might finally be behind the human race.

To discover otherwise shocked him likely as much as it did the rest of the people on Earth.

The shuttle landed and Captain Bradford disembarked, saluting the soldiers standing by the ramp. Vincent moved out to greet them and offered his own salute. "Welcome aboard, Captain. We're just about ready to get underway. Once we have some hyperspace coordinates, we'll be good to go."

"Thank you," Desmond said. "I'd like to introduce you to Agent Cassandra Alexander. Agent, this is Commander Vincent Bowman."

"A pleasure." Vincent shook her hand.

"Thank you, Commander." The Agent stepped back and admired the ships around them.

"If you'd all like to follow me, we've got quarters set up and Chief Engineer Webber would like a word with you before we depart." Vincent shrugged. "He has some concerns about the hyperdrive."

"Understood. I'll address him now." Desmond gestured to Salina. "You should take your post on the bridge. Cassie, you've got the coordinates so stow your things and get up there as well. Get Zach to program them in, do some predictive analysis and when I settle Nathaniel down, we'll get out of here."

"Yes, sir." Vincent gestured for Cassie to follow him. "Right this way."

"I'll see you both later," Salina said, heading off in another direction.

"So … the AIA." Vincent tried for some small talk. "I've never met a fully-fledged agent. Not that I'm aware of at least."

"We could be anywhere, that's true." Cassie grinned. "Though I can say there's less clandestine work going on in our own ships than you'd imagine. If it helps, this is the second time I've been on this ship. The first was long before it was commissioned. They barely had the life support systems working."

Vincent nodded. "I didn't come aboard until two weeks before our maiden voyage. That was a crash course in systems. Those of us who came on late had a lot of work to do, a ton to learn. Definitely worth it but challenging to say the least. Especially the more esoteric systems … like the hyperdrive."

"What is the engineer's concern?" Cassie asked. "Is he worried about the elemental mixtures or the distance we have to go?"

"As you probably know, no one's gone into hyperspace for more than an hour. We've heard rumors of a ten hour trip." Vincent shrugged. "Sounds pretty risky to me and I think the engineer just wants to voice his concerns to the captain. I'm surprised the doctor isn't in line to talk about it to be honest."

"Yes, I understand. Simulations suggest we won't notice." Cassie paused a moment. "But we both know real life and simulations aren't entirely fair comparisons, right?"

"Exactly." Vincent took her down a corridor and paused before an open door. "This is you. Please, make yourself at home."

The quarters were only a little smaller than his own with a bed, a desk and a refresher for getting cleaned up. She had enough room to have two people inside without it being cramped but not much more. Much of the crew had to live communally. These private rooms were reserved for VIPs and high ranking officers.

"Thank you," Cassie said. She dropped her things off. "Can you show me to the bridge? They hadn't designated where it would be when I was here last."

"Of course." Vincent gestured down the hall. "The elevator down here goes straight there. Just hop in it and take it to the top. It requires security clearance but I've already had you added to the system. It works on DNA."

"Nice." Cassie smiled. "I suppose we should go make history then, hm? Even if it will end with a fight."

"Indeed." Vincent sighed as they boarded the elevator. "So you're familiar with the alien's technology?"

"And ours," Cassie replied. "I've been hip deep in studying the Orb for several years now. The AIA has quite a few gadgets that came from it. I've got a bunch of them in my stuff. Hopefully, they'll come in handy but even if they don't, my computer's got some fantastic upgrades. I might be able to fashion them into something useful for the ship."

"I'm sure the engineers will be bothering you quite a bit," Vincent said. "They're always on the lookout for improvements. Hey, I had a question if you don't mind ... about the AIA."

"Go ahead, but we've only got a moment."

"Do you guys really learn all the crazy infiltration stuff? Hacking, fighting, you know ..."

Cassie nodded. "And we constantly have to practice, even when we're primarily assigned to research. They never know when one of us might have to go into the field and so we're always prepared. I honestly thought it was overkill until I got on that shuttle to come up here."

"Now?"

"I'm grateful they insisted I learn so much."

The doors opened and Vincent let her go first. Desmond had yet to arrive from his visit to engineering but the others bustled through their activities, preparing for departure. Vincent directed Cassie to a free station near Salina's. She already had a login to their network so she inserted her tablet into the dock and started typing.

He turned to his own reports, going through the checklist from other departments. Each section lead reported ready with only engineering appearing red on the list. Vincent expected as much and wondered how the captain would fare with Nathaniel. They didn't have a choice, so one way or another, they would be on their way shortly. Complaining merely delayed things.

***

Desmond arrived in engineering and Lieutenant Commander Nathaniel Webber immediately met him at the door. He was a bald man, short at five-eight but he carried himself with a lot of feisty dignity. The neat goatee gave him a tough look but at forty-seven, he'd long since given up any sort of trouble off duty.

"What's going on, Nathaniel?" Desmond asked. "We have to get moving. The orders came from the council."

"I understand, Captain, but we've got to take a moment before we just dive into this. The hyperdrive's been tested, yes … but I'm not sure what's going to happen if we put ourselves into a long-distance trip of ten hours."

"What do the simulations say?"

Nathaniel waved his hand at him. "You know as well as I do what those are good for." He motioned for him to follow him. "Come into my office for a moment." They entered the private room before the engineer continued his argument. "What if we melt down?"

"What're the chances of that and how paranoid are you being?" Desmond held his hand up. "The question is, do you honestly think that there's a danger or are you simply being overly cautious? Because right now, after what happened, we don't have the luxury of waiting around for more testing. We have to go. Now."

Nathaniel nearly answered immediately but he stopped himself and took a deep breath. "Okay, I'm just being overly cautious but I think I've got good cause."

"All I can ask you to do is ensure you've taken every safety precaution possible." Desmond smiled. "Beyond that, we're going to be playing a little fate. I'm pretty confident that it's not going to be any different going all the way out there than it was to return home from our first trip. Think about it. The system is designed for this."

"I know … and I don't mean to be the one to cry wolf before we've even seen some fur …" Nathaniel ran his hand over his head and nodded. "I'll make sure we get there. Somehow and no matter what, we'll make it."

"Look on the bright side, we have an AIA agent on board and she's studied all this stuff. From what I've been led to believe, her understanding of our systems is second to none. You'll be able to tap into her experience just after we take off. Maybe she can help and she's got the data we took from the aliens."

"And we have access to it?"

Desmond nodded. "All of it. She's on full share mode so take advantage while you can. You know how the AIA can be."

"Not really, no … but I'll definitely reach out to her." Nathaniel stood up straighter. "Alright, Captain. I'll sign off and we'll get out of here. Thanks for the quick talk. I appreciate it."

"I understand and thank you for not pushing back until I had to give you a direct order." Desmond patted him on the shoulder. "It's time to see what your ship can do, Lieutenant Commander Webber. Can you fire up the hyperdrive as we input some coordinates taking us far beyond where any human has even thought to go?"

"Yes, sir … I do believe I can."

□

Chapter 5

Desmond returned to the bridge and paused just inside the door, taking a look at the officers working at their stations. Zach glanced back and called out, "Captain on the bridge." This drew the attention of the others and Desmond raised a hand, letting them know to continue what they were doing.

He took his seat and leaned over to Vincent. "Are we ready to go? Nathaniel should've signed off."

"He did, sir. Agent Alexander has provided the coordinates to our destination and she's working with Salina on the final predictive analysis before we depart. We're ready to leave Earth's orbit on your command and we should be able to initiate hyperspace within twenty minutes after that."

Desmond frowned and nodded. "Okay. Zach, take us out of orbit. Salina, get me a com to Admiral Reach, please. Priority Two."

Established communication protocols put together five major priorities. They ranged from not at all urgent (five) to there's a major disaster occurring (one). The most commonly used option was three which allowed the recipient of the contact to finish whatever they were doing before accepting the contact.

Two meant they needed to speak right away but there was no emergency currently happening.

"Yes, sir." Salina tapped her touch screen several times before announcing, "You are connected."

"Admiral, this is Captain Bradford and we are leaving orbit now. Any last orders?"

"Come back alive, Desmond. We need your ship and your crew. If you don't think you can take the enemy, get your asses back here and report in. Understood?"

"Loud and clear, sir." Desmond smiled. "We'll talk soon. Close channel and alert the ship that we will be entering hyperspace in approximately twenty minutes."

Cassie spoke quietly to Salina but the bridge was really too small not to hear her. "Is it really so jarring? I mean, I've only read about the simulations. You guys have actually done it. Do people need to brace and all that?"

"For the initial entry," Salina said, "yes, we do. Once we've established ourselves, movement about the ship is normal. We haven't encountered any turbulence while in FTL. However, we didn't really go that far."

"I see." Cassie cleared her throat. "Here's to new experiences, huh?"

The ship's engines kicked on and the hull vibrated ever so slightly. Earth occupied the majority of the view screen for a brief moment and then it did not. They peered into deep space, moving swiftly away from their home. The next stars out there would be totally unfamiliar with new patterns to catalog.

If only we were going for such a peaceful reason. Desmond, like the rest of the crew, looked forward to seeing the rest of the universe. He studied to be a soldier but he always thought it would be an unnecessary precaution. Racing to stop another species never crossed his mind. Had someone warned him about an invasion, he would've thought they were crazy.

He wondered about Agent Alexander, how she would fare on this mission. She supposedly underwent some pretty intense training to get where she was, both physical and mental. Desmond never really thought about the AIA so he didn't feel inclined not to trust her simply because of her chosen career path.

Others might not be so easy going. The only thing anyone knew about the AIA involved rumors. They were shadowy though public enough to know It. This made them scarier to the right kind of people, those who liked to explore conspiracy theories. Some people aboard would likely have questions for her about what she did.

Desmond just wanted to know that she could do her job and maintain a calm disposition. So far, she'd proven to be pretty amazing. Getting into the alien computers and extracting the data couldn't have been easy. It proved she knew what she was doing, that she had the training she spoke of and moreover, she applied it brilliantly.

That unto itself gave him confidence in her abilities. He'd need to take a few minutes to talk to her when they were fully underway, maybe get to know where she was coming from. If she had any disadvantage at all, it was a lack of time in space. But as with all things, a little time and experience went a long way.

Cassie would be fine if not by the time they arrived, then shortly after.

"We are nearly in position to engage hyperdrive," Zach said. "Predictive analysis?"

"Complete," Salina said. "I've sent a minor adjustment to your course and it's been verified by Agent Alexander. Please confirm."

Zach took a moment and nodded. "Confirmed. I'm ready to initiate hyperspace on your mark, Captain."

Desmond paused for a moment, preparing himself for the biggest order of his career. When he told his pilot to send them hurtling through space to another solar system, he would be taking another giant step for mankind. This one came with so many repercussions. First, they'd know they could do it and second, they'd find out if they could hold their own against the aliens.

Again. This might be an easier fight depending on what we find there.

"Engage." He spoke the word firmly, but hoped he didn't put too much energy behind it. Too much passion or emotion wouldn't do anyone any good. He needed to be the picture of calm and he intended to stay that way even if his insides were dancing. "Let's see what's at the other end of this adventure."

Zach nodded once before tapping the controls. The ship began to hum and a low whine began to build deep within the ship. Desmond sat back in his chair and drew a deep breath, forcing himself not to grip the chair arms tightly. They'd been through this twice before, once to get to the edge of their solar system and once to come back to battle the aliens.

A third time shouldn't have affected him at all but he couldn't pretend to be inhuman. This new technology might not work in a spectacular fashion. It may simply fail at best or flat out explode. The screen went dark as the ship shimmered out of their reality as they knew it and into the alternate dimension of hyperspace.

Desmond always had a problem accepting the explanation he was given about hyperspace. He preferred to think of it as the ship simply going very fast but they insisted that they were shifting beyond the natural realm where certainly rules did not apply. This allowed them to race along without killing everyone on board.

Technically, the ship was simply moving at maximum speed but in this other space, they were able to cover up to twenty times the distance. A trip to the outer edge of their space, at a reasonable speed, took about forty minutes. When they raced back at three-quarters full, they got back in half that.

Now they'd be moving at full speed and it would still take several hours. The time depended on all the small corrections the ship's computer would make along the way and so it would be variable. Such a trip might've taken twenty hours under a different set of circumstances.

Researchers suggested they'd be able to better predict these things with further trials. The Gnosis was performing those tests now, in production. Salina was recording everything about the ship during the flight. Engine performance, structural integrity, circuitry decay and crew efficiency all went into a massive database to be studied at a later time.

They shut off the exterior cameras and went to sensors only. This meant the view screen stopped showing outside and instead began displaying internal system monitoring. The initial plunge made the ship rattle for a moment but it smoothed out quickly, just as before. Tension on the bridge increased dramatically until Salina spoke up.

"All systems read normal. We are now in hyperspace."

Zach clapped his hands and hooted. "Amazing! I knew this complicated mess would hold together!"

"Was that a concern?" Cassie asked. "Were you guys worried something would happen?"

"It's only the third time we've done it," Vincent replied. "So I think people were a bit nervous."

Cassie nodded and returned to what she was doing, her eyes wide.

Desmond stood and began giving orders. "Alright, Zach, I want Deacon up here to relieve you while we're in hyperspace. When we arrive, you've got to be back on duty. Get some food and downtime. You'll need it. Vincent, work with Dennis to ensure the pilots are ready when we arrive. They should also get some rest. Same with the marines."

"I'm on it, sir." Vincent got on his com and started making connections.

"Agent Alexander, I believe Salina, you and I have something to discuss in regards to these ships. I'd like a quick briefing that we can disseminate to the other section heads as soon as possible. Then everyone gets a few hours downtime before we arrive and have to be awake for God knows how long." Desmond took a breath and clapped his hands. "Ready?"

A round of affirmatives filled the room.

"Then I'll get out of your hair to make it happen."

***

Cassie expected the alien technology briefing to be a hyper-efficient affair with direct questions and severity but Desmond surprised her. He kept the meeting pleasant and though they discussed sensitive, serious topics, he didn't allow it to become a brooding exploration into the capabilities of their enemies. She admired how easy it was to talk in his presence.

Salina, on the other hand, remained just as down to business as she had been during their time on Earth together. She held valuable insights into the situation and offered tactical advice throughout the discussion. After an hour of exploring their own research data and what they found in the alien computers, she proved to have a near photographic memory.

"Let me sum up," Desmond said, "they've got shields like ours but they have a better understanding of how to modulate them to greater effect, right?"

Cassie nodded. "Yes, I've been trying to find a way to make ours do the same but I'll need to speak with an engineer so I don't design something beyond system specs. I know we're able to do it but we have to do so in a way that won't burn out existing components."

"Okay." Desmond made a note on his tablet before continuing. "We also know their weapons are on par with ours except for the strange sphere thing they used toward the end of the engagement. Any theories on why they waited so long?"

"Extreme power drain," Salina said. "All my readings indicate they were essentially useless for at least a minute after it happened. Had we not attacked so quickly, it might've even taken them longer to recover."

"Sounds like a parting shot to me." Desmond rubbed his chin, staring into space. "Maybe that ship was trying to sacrifice itself to give the others a chance to finish their assignments."

"They didn't know we could get back so quickly," Salina pointed out. "After all, they waited to attack until we were as far away as we would get."

"None of them knew where you were going either," Cassie added. "You might've still been in hyperspace when they made their move."

"Great points." Desmond made another note. "Armor similar to ours … Maneuverability, slightly better on the smaller ships and their fighters … Well, they didn't turn out to be as scary as Salina predicted."

"No," Salina conceded, "but they do have an enhanced form of inertial dampeners … either that or their pilots are simply conditioned to heavier G-force. Their maneuvers were pretty spectacular and I know all of our pilots have studied the data exhaustively. They'll be ready for their next engagement."

"Good. I'm glad to hear it." Desmond gestured to the screen again. "Have we figured out their communications yet? Can we jam them or at least interfere with their ability to chat?"

Cassie fielded the question. "I can't say yes for sure yet but I've been working on it. Whether I'll have an application ready for this next conflict, it's hard to say. Our normal methods wouldn't work though. They use a lot of energy to ensure their coms function, however. This gives us an advantage because I think I can intercept them."

"I'd love to see how you intend to," Salina said. "Imagine how much easier this fight will be if we're able to monitor their coms."

Desmond smirked before saying, "It won't matter much if they know about it. Are we going to be able to do this without alerting them?"

Cassie shrugged. "Unfortunately, the documentation we have from them doesn't really dive into their scanning abilities. If they have a mature sensor and monitoring system, we might not be able to but if we're throwing all kinds of frequencies around, jamming and such, then who knows how far we can go?"

"They'd be so busy cleaning up our interference," Salina said, "they may not notice we're listening."

"I like it," Desmond replied. "Okay, so I'm going to give this briefing to the others. You will both be present in case of any technical questions. When we're done, I'll have Cassie work with Nathaniel to check on the shield modulation but don't put too much time into it. You need to get some rest and we've only got nine hours left to get everything done."

"Understood," Cassie replied. "Do we need to talk about anything else?"

"No, I've got all the data here and I've asked the extra questions I had." Desmond stood. "We'll meet up in the briefing room to finish. Thank you both for compiling all this. It's going to make a huge difference. Believe me."

***

The briefing didn't take long and Cassie gathered her things for a trip down to engineering. Chief Engineer Webber had attended the meeting but he left immediately along with the others. They all asked sensible questions, taking their briefings back to share with their people. None of them seemed nervous about the prospect of their assignment.

Perhaps they were simply too professional to show any sort of fear around their peers.

Desmond stepped close, speaking quietly. "Do you mind if I escort you to engineering? I'd like a word as we go."

"Yes, Mister Webber already left and I was hoping he'd remind me of how to get there. When I visited the ship last, there weren't as many walls."

Desmond grinned. "Would've been a lot easier to get around, that's for sure. Come on."

Cassie fell into step beside him, admiring the aesthetic they gave the place. It felt far less utilitarian than when she had visited it, more like a home. The intent was to ensure people didn't feel like cogs in a machine. It was important for every crew member to have a sense of comfort, especially on a long space voyage.

"So, I know you're from California and that you went to Geneva for school," Desmond started. "What're your hobbies, Agent?"

"Oh um … Well …" Cassie blushed. "I've always been really good with computers but I really love music. So when I'm not swamped, I write songs. Electronic stuff mostly 'cause I can't play an instrument, but programming beats and stuff? No problem. Living in Europe also means I had access to great performers."

"Music lover." Desmond smiled. "That helps to offset the image of an AIA agent essentially being a work machine that lives in the shadows of conspiracy."

"No, we're not like that." Cassie scratched her head. "But I get the misunderstanding. It's not like we're transparent about our activities. Classified information tends to make us all a bit twitchy to share things. Still, I can assure you my colleagues are all quite normal with their different passions and extracurricular activities. No one lives in the office. Not all the time."

"But it's a busy job."

"Of course, there's a lot of work to do. Sixty-hour weeks are the norm but if we're there longer, it's the exception to the rule." Cassie chuckled. "Of course, now that I'm here I suppose we'll be working during waking hours."

"No, we work by six hour shifts, with four going to make up what we call a cluster, or day. Traditionally, we work a full six hour shift at whatever our standard duty is, take a shift for training or maintenance then have the other two off for sleep and recreation. Time is maximized and people have a chance to unwind without the threat of being back on in a few hours."

"I hadn't read about that," Cassie said. "Sounds like it'll work okay. We're a lot more flexible at the AIA but then again, we're not running the thing we're living on." She paused. "What about you? What're your hobbies? Even if I only gave you one of mine."

"I'm sure I'll get more out of you later," Desmond replied. "I'm a reader. Love classics. The fact we've got the Library of Congress loaded onto the computers here makes me very happy. That's how I unwind. Grab something I haven't read yet and lose myself for a while. I always sleep best after I've devoured a couple chapters."

"You sure that's not because they're boring?" Cassie smiled to show the question was a joke. "That you're reading stuffy material?"

Desmond chuckled. "Pretty sure. I'll let you know the next time I settle down for a shift." He paused at a door. "This is engineering. Nathaniel's a good man, but know he can be … stubborn. Good luck with the shields and be sure to get some rest before we arrive. You're going to want to be at your best during whatever happens."

"One more thing ..." Cassie took him a few steps away, lowering her voice. "It involves protocol. I don't want there to be any confusion about my presence aboard your ship. I recognize I'm a civilian but until otherwise stated, I am referring to you as my direct superior. I'll do my best to speak appropriately with 'sir' and all that but do forgive me if I slip."

"Admiral Reach warned me about the AIA," Desmond replied. "He told me you folks like to take operational command on occasion. I'm glad to hear you haven't been given such an order. I'm not worried about you, Agent Alexander. So far, you seem to be in this for the right reasons and you've been nothing but honest and helpful. Thanks for the quick talk."

"See you back on the bridge later then," Cassie called after him as he walked away. He waved and she took a quick breath before turning back to Engineering. She tapped the panel and opened the door, stepping into a noisy technological wonderland she had only read about prior to boarding the ship.

Panels lined the walls and several small maintenance corridors led off to different parts of the ship for fine, manual work. Much of the Gnosis could be repaired right from the center of engineering Cassie was standing in. The automated systems were incredible but occasionally, people needed to be involved. They could make their way to any part of the ship from there.

When she first saw how much access those tunnels had, the security part of her became nervous. If unauthorized personnel got in there, they could access any part of the ship. They got around it with DNA coding. If someone entered a section, doors would close trapping them inside.

These sensors were not linked to the central computer and so could not be hacked without getting into one of the tunnels. Even then, by the time the person got in there and started their mischief, they'd already be caught. It sounded foolproof but when they had time, Cassie intended to see about bolstering the security even more.

Nathaniel Webber approached her, all smiles. He didn't seem particularly pleased to see her despite the outward expression. She got the impression he felt her contribution would be unneeded and maybe he was right. One of the most important lessons she learned with the AIA was to never believe she was the sole person who could handle a problem.

Two sets of eyes were always better than one when it came to a problem after all. She hoped to impart this to the stubborn engineer.

"Welcome," Nathaniel said. "This is where the magic happens. I'll be honest and frank, Miss Alexander. I'm not sure what you'll be able to do down here that I haven't already been able to accomplish with my own people."

Miss again. I must look like a child or something. Cassie put on a smile to mask her annoyance. "I'm hoping I can offer some inspiration more than anything. I've brought some data I'd like to share and compare with our current setup. With any luck, the two of us can determine whether it's useful and can be implemented or if it's incompatible."

"I see." Nathaniel narrowed his eyes. "This is the frequency modifications discussed during the briefing, right?"

Cassie nodded. "Exactly. That's how the enemy works their defenses."

"I've already thought about it." Nathaniel led her over to his terminal and tapped at the screen. He brought up the shield array system. "One of the early problems we managed to overcome with this ship involved evenly distributing power to all systems during heavy usage. Combat situations are the worst.

"When we're powering the engines for maneuverability, weapons, shields and maintaining life support, we're taxing the generators." Nathaniel changed the screen to show the power relays. "Allowing the shields to cycle would essentially be like rebooting them over and over again, which would put a heavier draw on power."

Cassie scrutinized his screen for several moments before pulling out her tablet and tapping away. The problem he spoke of had been addressed by the aliens but it may have been by design. Still, the way he described the act sounded terribly inefficient and certainly something they should have been able to account for.

The shield system on the Gnosis was built like a brick wall. The idea was to harden it so much it would deflect mass driver weapons easily and energy weapons would simply not be powerful enough to punch through. This was an old way of thinking. As she read through the way the enemy shields worked, she noted the key difference.

They enabled their defenses to be flexible. Their shields reacted to attacks rather than just sat there waiting for one. An energy blast would be absorbed and mass drivers would be stopped though perhaps not as efficiently. That was their primary weakness. Combining their method and the way the Gnosis currently operated would be the best of both worlds.

Cassie showed Nathaniel her tablet and explained what she saw, inviting him to educate her. By deferring to his expertise, she felt him coming around. His standoffish first impression might've been all stubbornness or maybe he worried she'd try to pull rank. Whatever problem he had with her to begin with melted away the deeper they delved into the alien technology.

"The problem I see," Cassie said, "is our focus on the energy wall versus a fluid deflection."

"Altering our system won't be simple," Nathaniel replied. "But it can be done without a complete overhaul. It comes down to modifying the emitters and how they regulate the energy before creating the field. Unfortunately, we can't make this happen while in hyperspace because we can't properly test it. Nor can we do it when we arrive 'cause we'll likely need the shields up."

Cassie nodded. "Major system changes like this wouldn't work in the field without an absolute necessity. However, there's a minor change I'd like you to consider in regards to their sphere weapon. As you know, it nudged the Gnosis even at range. I have two proposals but one of them isn't as practical."

"Go ahead."

"On one hand, Lieutenant Gold discovered the energy reading and the pilot got the ship out of range quickly. If we're going to go with a retreat action, then we need a quicker tie-in with engineering so we can divert more power to the engines. An overdrive if you will. That should give us the boost we need to avoid any damage at all."

"Could work, yes. Though if I know the captain, he won't want to withdraw next time. What's your other thought?"

"We can attempt to match the frequency with our shields to do what they did while avoiding damage."

Nathaniel shook his head. "Too risky. Without the ability to test, if we failed, we'd take the full brunt. I have a third option but it involves some of your fancy applications."

"Oh?"

"You cracked their computer code so you understand how their security works. If you prepare ahead of time, you might be able to jam their system and delay the release of the weapon." Nathaniel brought up a simulation and showed how such a thing might work. "You could do anything from prevent the attack to destroying their reactor."

Cassie really looked at his proposal, considering how best to go about it. Sending a message to the ship telling it to delay release would definitely send a power surge throughout the system. Depending on their safety protocols, it would likely only short out some of their panels but the result would come down to the weapon not discharging.

"I'll need to play around with it but I've got the data necessary in my computer." Cassie frowned in thought. "Yes, that's doable."

"While you take care of that, I'll see what can be done to tweak our shields without compromising functionality. At least this time, we'll have to go with what we've got. If only we had a little more time …"

Cassie nodded. "We can't afford delays. It may already be too late. Depending on what opposition the enemy has uncovered, of course."

Nathaniel turned back to his terminal. "All we can do is be ready this time and the next. Good luck, Miss Alexander. I look forward to working with you more."

As she left engineering, Cassie felt good about the contacts she was making with the different department heads on the ship. Commander Bowman seemed okay as did Lieutenant Gold. Winning over Nathaniel helped a lot and she only had a couple more to go. Undoubtedly, she'd have her chance to talk to them before the first mission concluded.

But just then, she needed to work on the jamming application. She might not get the rest she needed after all but at least they'd have a fighting chance against the spherical weapon. Would their gathered intelligence be enough to turn the tide of a battle? The aliens had time to study them as well.

This might come down to who did the best research. Of course, they can't possibly anticipate we'll be able to follow them. After all, they were convinced humanity would be a push over. They divided their force as a result. The audacity of sending a single ship might be intimidating … or it could be the single worst idea we've come up with.

Time would tell if Earth made the right call in pursuing the enemy and involving themselves in galactic affairs, such as they were. The enemy databases didn't speak about other races out in space, other civilizations beyond their own. Perhaps if one of their ship's computers would've survived, more comprehensive data would've been available.

As such, they had to learn a few things on their own. Cassie believed the Gnosis was ready for such an adventure. Now they simply had to survive it to benefit from the spoils.

☐

Chapter 6

Desmond returned to the bridge when they were about to emerge from hyperspace. The calculation suggested thirty minutes and he needed some time to address the crew and prepare. Pilots boarded their fighters and bombers, marines filed down to the shuttles and the Gnosis felt on the verge of bursting from barely contained adrenaline.

Zach relieved Deacon, the last of the primary bridge crew to take his seat. Those with the most experience took their posts and each department head sounded off their readiness. Desmond noted they were green across the board. When they arrived, all units would be as prepared for combat as possible.

Desmond received the report from Nathaniel that they were unable to make significant modifications to the shields. This was not unexpected news but it did disappoint him. The information went on to state that Cassandra may have found a way to disrupt the spherical attack. There was no indication she'd succeeded yet.

"Agent Alexander," Desmond said. "Nathaniel stated you were working on some kind of app to jam an enemy attack. Have you had any luck?"

"I wrote an application and tested it against their security protocols. Hardened systems will be a challenge but I'm confident I can at least delay their special weapon long enough for us to gain some distance." Cassie paused. "I just finished another simulation. If I can get more experience with some of their active defenses, I'll be able to improve this significantly."

"Excellent." Desmond glanced at the chronometer. They had ten minutes to go. Butterflies hit his stomach but he was able to quell them with a deep breath. When he left his quarters and headed to the bridge, he felt the tension building in the ship. He didn't sense fear per se but more anticipation. They wanted to get into the action.

Ten hours was a long time to think about a fight.

Desmond spent the next few moments going through minor reports, issues that didn't demand immediate attention. After the third one, Zach called out that they had two minutes before emerging. He turned the screen to tactical in preparation for what was to come. The countdown began at thirty seconds and when he reached zero, the main screen changed to a frontal view.

The ship shuddered for a moment, shaking from the re-entry into real space. Lights flickered then remained steady. Zach's hands flew over his controls and as he applied retro thrusters, Desmond felt a hint of pressure as the inertial dampeners fought to keep up with the suddenness of their motion.

"Checking position," Salina announced. "We have arrived within ten-thousand kilometers of our intended coordinates."

"Fantastic job, everyone," Desmond said. "That's pretty damn impressive. Now, to the business at hand. System scan?"

Salina hummed. "The system rebooted when we came out of hyperspace. It's almost back up but that's … odd."

"Wait," Cassie jumped in. "Oh, I see what happened. When the lights flickered, we experienced a power surge. Several systems have been rebooted. I can work with engineering right now to find out if there's a short in the relay … If you don't mind."

Desmond nodded. "Please do. Let's get a quick diagnostic on all essential systems. If something happened on that re-entry, we want to know before we need those things. Vincent, have the pilots ready to launch at a moment's notice. Make every moment count, people. They don't have the disadvantage of a reboot so if they're out there, they know we're here by now."

Desmond stood and joined Salina at her station, watching the progress meter fill as the system came back online. He wondered if there was simply a glitch or if the distance itself had something to do with it. There was no precedent to base an opinion on, only simulation data and two short trips.

The after-action briefings would involve a lot of questions.

Salina began tapping at her console the moment the system came back online and put her findings on the main screen. Desmond turned to look at the data. Eight planets surrounded a star much like Sol. Hard and fast scans showed the fourth planet was the closest to Earth standards with only slightly lighter gravity and an identical oxygen content.

We've talked about the Goldilocks planet before but I never thought we'd find one on our first trip out. Of course, I have to give the aliens the credit in this case. We're merely following them, not discovering on our own.

"Multiple ships discovered," Salina said. She motioned for Cassie to join her. "Look at those. There are five of the alien ships, we expected those but what about these? I don't even know what to call them but they're definitely inorganic. What do you make of them?"

"Different types of aliens," Cassie replied. "The inhabitants of the planet they're invading perhaps. They … seem to be in conflict."

"Maybe we can get them on the com and tell them we're here to help," Desmond suggested. "Hail them."

"I'm afraid they're unmanned, sir." Salina tapped at her console and nodded. "Yes, they are definitely unmanned and are coming from that larger, dome like structure orbiting the planet. It's some kind of defensive platform sending out these drones. No life forms in there either. It's totally automated."

"Great." Desmond sighed. "Means they won't be friendly to us either. How big are the drones?"

Salina replied, "Small. They appear to be fighter size. In fact, that's what the enemy is using to fight them but … they must've been at this for a while. There's debris in orbit … The alien ships."

"Estimated number?" Desmond asked.

"More than five," Cassie answered. "But there's plenty of debris from the indigenous technology as well. I'd be willing to guess there were a lot more of those orbital defenses before and now they're down to two."

Salina added, "Surface scans show a smaller scout vessel landed and a contingency of alien ground forces are converging on a structure but there is weapon's fire. I'm not sure what they're fighting. There's life on the surface but it isn't like Earth. No large congregations that would indicate cities. Just structures. Abandoned …" She turned to Desmond. "Or dead."

Desmond rubbed his chin and turned to his own screen, checking the diagnostic reports. They indicated all systems were operational. Cassie and Nathaniel had another test running, checking what might've caused the short but they hadn't found it yet. They didn't have time to thoroughly investigate everything before jumping into action.

"Zach, get us closer." Desmond sat down. "Vincent, when we're within range, launch all fighters. Raptor's on escort. Get the marines down to the ground and prevent the enemy from doing whatever they're doing. Tell them to be prepared for a serious fight … possibly from two groups."

Affirmatives rang through the bridge and the ship's thrusters ignited. Shields were raised and weapons powered on. As they advanced, they received additional information about the conflict raging ahead of them. The indigenous defense platforms showed massive energy readings. Powerful shields protected them but something else happened inside.

Salina's deep scan of the structure showed the vast majority of it was dedicated to manufacturing the drones. The entire thing was automated, leaving only enough room for a reactor which generated an enormous amount of energy, especially considering it was solar powered.

The efficiency of the platform was incredible as each subsection built a piece of the drones, churning them out quickly enough to constantly reinforce their numbers. As a result, it would've been very difficult to gain a beachhead in the planet's orbit and further explained why the aliens lost vessels and hadn't achieved their own objectives yet.

They may have only gotten this far because they studied their adversaries like us. Every moment of delay they had gave us time to arrive and intervene.

"Try to get the aliens on com," Desmond said. "Maybe we can make this exchange peaceful."

Salina spoke into her microphone with several different messages, tapping her screen every few moments. She finally shook her head. "I'm getting nothing but static on all frequencies, sir."

"Understood." Desmond gestured to Vincent. "Launch the fighters and have them engage immediately. Anything that shoots back. Rules of engagement are wide open. For the marines, have them try to identify friendly organic targets. Everything else is fair game. Prioritize their lives above all else. I want everyone getting home after this mission."

"We will be in range to fire in less than three minutes," Zach said. "What're my target priorities?"

Desmond hesitated to answer. On one hand, he felt like the defense platforms should be their first order of business. They weren't going to stop generating drones to fight off invaders but on the other hand, attacking the aliens meant they would have to defend themselves on two fronts. They might make easier work of the remaining vessels with the help.

An idea hit him and he turned back to Vincent. "Get our bombers out there. I want those platforms taken down by them. The fighters focus on the fight close at hand and we'll aim for the alien capital ships. Zach, target the nearest ship. We'll go from there."

"Yes, sir. I'm on it now."

"Okay, this is it." Desmond glanced back at Cassie. "Agent Alexander, I hope you're ready in case they try their special attack. Beyond that, this is looking pretty straightforward, folks. Frequent reports from all parties away from the ship filtered through Commander Bowman. Here we go. Make your efforts count."

***

Lieutenant Kate Zeller began flying when she was old enough to see over the controls of her father's antique crop duster. They'd long been out of use but she learned to operate the thing and never looked back. Joining the military gave her an opportunity to do what she loved the most, only faster.

Sitting behind the controls of a fighter provided her with the most intense outlet for her need to push the envelope, to pit herself not only against an opponent but her own skills as well. As the other pilots in Mustang Squadron launched, she tapped her foot in anticipation. When finally she got the green light, she gunned the throttle, jetting out into open space.

The challenge of a strange enemy so far from home further appealed to her competitive nature. No one else from Earth could boast what they were about to do and she fully intended to make the most of the experience. If these aliens decided to truly start a war, they did not understand what door they opened.

A last minute briefing let them know about the kink in the chain. The automated defenses protecting the planet sounded pretty nasty. They were already engaged with the aliens and would have to be dealt with before the Gnosis could safely take orbit. Bombers were en route and were being escorted by Charger squadron.

Kate checked out her scanner, bringing up the data on the drones. They were smaller than the Earth ships but not by much. Their hulls were dedicated to thrusters, allowing them precise maneuverability, and weapons. Each unit boasted energy weapons, tough enough that the computer suggested caution when engaging.

It's never good when the computer issues an actual warning, Kate thought. Luckily, their own defenses are subpar at best.

Indeed, they only seemed to be surrounded by environmental shields which wouldn't stop a solid hit from any weapon really. They relied on maneuverability and numbers to take down threats and considering the briefing said additional drones were constantly being replicated, it made sense.

If the people on this planet had a ship like the Gnosis as well, they could defend their home indefinitely.

And yet they don't even seem to be here. What happened on this planet? Lord, I bet the marines are going to find out.

"Listen up folks," Denis's voice filled her helmet. "We are within range. Break off with your wingmen and engage. Prioritize the aliens. They represent the greater threat. Any questions?" No one spoke up. "Then get to it."

Kate's wingman was Lieutenant Hal Brown. He'd been shot down in the last engagement and she felt somewhat responsible. Once they met up in the medical bay, he exonerated her immediately. He claimed he had been too aggressive and maybe he was right. They didn't know what they were dealing with and he went straight for the throat.

"You ready?" Kate asked. "I'll take lead."

"Go for it," Hal replied. "And I'm one hundred percent ready. Believe me, I had a lot of time to think about these guys while I waited for search and rescue."

Kate winced. I bet he did. Hal flew on her right and she pushed ahead of him, taking the lead. He gave her some space as she enhanced her HUD, specifically the targeting system. The amber reticle had tiny lines branching off, touching squares that surrounded several enemy fighters. They plotted distance, speed and fed additional information back to the computer.

The ship rumbled from the speed. Inertial dampeners worked hard but they weren't enough to fend off all the g-force, which pressed her into her seat. Her shoulders began to ache, a familiar sensation she'd grown to associate with her passion. It didn't bother her anymore. A little pain allowed her to maintain a feel of the ship, giving her a physical connection to it.

Kate's first target closed to within range. She engaged the side thrusters, nudging her to the left just enough for a better firing solution. The enemy flew wildly to avoid a couple drones, which buzzed around it with all the maneuverability of bees swarming around their hive. They were so close, they'd probably take splash damage from any explosions.

Stray shots blurred by, purple beams streaking off into the distance. Something clipped Kate's shields, making them flare briefly. The HUD showed no appreciable damage. She narrowed her eyes and fired her mass drivers. As the guns erupted to her left and right, the vessel reacted with tiny vibrations through the frame.

Had she not been so familiar with the workings of the fighter, she might not have even noticed.

The first spread missed cleanly but as she fired a second time, a couple of the metal shards connected with one of the drones. An entire side of the small craft popped off and it tumbled, a bout of orange energy billowing from the hull before exploding some distance away. The other drone didn't even hesitate and continued its assault.

The alien's shields continued to flare, each shot not quite enough to get through on their own but with the constant hammering, the defenses wouldn't last. Despite some pretty impressive evasion attempts, the alien couldn't shake his opponent and none of his friends were close enough to help.

Hal fired his beam weapons, striking the alien ship dead on the side. The shields lit up far brighter than what the drone had managed. Kate took advantage of the hit and blasted away at him. She was closing fast though and had time for one attack before having to evade or risk slamming into the target.

Their movements may have been erratic but they weren't going anywhere. Their dogfight kept them contained to a fairly small area. Kate's attack grazed the rear of her target and she veered off just as the drone let loose another flurry. The computer began to buzz, an indication that the defenses for her target were down.

Kate glanced over her shoulder in time to see pieces of its hull chipped away by the drone. She came around, trying for a better firing solution and Hal kept to her tail, moving with her. The alien dove, a swift direction change that might've broken bones even with solid inertial dampeners.

Finally, the drone seemed to overshoot him, giving the alien a second to breathe.

Hal called out, "I've got a lock. Firing." Several rounds from his mass drivers filled the air and Kate pulled up to give him some room. The enemy veered but chose the wrong direction, taking a full volley right on the top of his ship. Lights winked out on the target, the engines went dark and the pilot ejected a moment before his ship burst in all directions.

The drone spun in place and came straight at Kate, rapidly firing energy bolts in her direction. Several shots riddled her shields before she could roll to the side, avoiding the last of them. It flew by her, adjusting course and coming back around for another firing solution. She considered it for a brief moment before speaking up.

"We can't keep a tight formation with that thing. Break and get an angle."

"That won't work when there's more than one," Hal said.

"I get that but hey, we've got time to worry about that later, right?"

Hal chuckled. "I guess … but not much. Okay, breaking now."

They separated, giving themselves some distance as the attacking drone made another pass. This time, it flew between them from behind. Kate took the opportunity and fired but the drone flipped away, casually evading the attack. Hal fired as well and cursed over the com. "I had target lock on that thing!"

Time to try something new. Kate redirected herself, flipping around in such an extreme maneuver, her entire body felt like it was being crushed. The moment she had the drone in her sites, she went for lock, ignoring the ache in every bone. Tone buzzed and she fired a missile, hoping her AI could outfly her opponent.

The projectile started chasing the target and they zoomed off toward the others. It's getting help! "Do you see that, Hal?"

"Yes, those things are terrifying."

"Look out!" Hal's warning came a moment too late as a beam weapon directly hit her after-shields. She maneuvered out of the way, letting one of the enemy alien ships fly by. It banked and came around, firing at Hal. He returned fire, tilting his ship to avoid their attack. The two nearly collided as they went by one another.

Kate redirected to fly after it but another ship came at her. "Hal, I've got one on me now too. We need to form up."

"I'm a little busy. Rendezvous at the coordinates I'm sending you right now." Her computer put a waypoint on her HUD. "Fight your way there."

"On it."

Banking hard left, she reversed the maneuver at the last second and once again put herself through some serious pain. The inertial dampeners screamed as she turned but the ploy worked. Her opponent bought the first maneuver and didn't bother to redirect. This gave her a fantastic firing solution and she let loose a volley of ammo before following up with beams.

The alien didn't have the chance to dodge before taking both attacks. The energy beams hit first, cutting through the shields and the mass drivers ripped up the engines. Kate's target turned on its good engine, trying to limp off. She pulled up and fired again, finishing him off before spinning around to join Hal.

"This is Mustang One," Denis announced over the com. "We're being overwhelmed over here. Need some backup."

"You got yours, Hal?" Kate asked. "We need to go."

"Mine's bugging out but I can get him ..." Hal hummed. "I'm breaking off. We'll regroup on Mustang One. How're you holding up?"

Kate checked and all systems were normal. Shields were not quite to one hundred percent after her near misses but they were recharging. Automated repair systems engaged, enhancing the relays to ensure power made it to weapons and shields equally. She made a minor adjustment, manually giving the shields some more.

"I'm good," Kate announced. "I'll follow your lead."

***

Cassie probed the enemy security protocols, attempting to establish a link to them with their own technology. She had just enough information to make it seem possible but each failure started to get frustrating. There were so many benefits to breaking through their defenses, not the least of which might be the chance for diplomacy.

I'd love to get into their coms. Even if they don't want to talk to us directly, we might be able to hear them.

Getting through also meant her application would work to delay or even stop the enemies from using their special weapon. To that point, they hadn't seen them try it but then the Gnosis had yet to truly open fire. They were closing in but the drones seemed to be giving them quite the run for their money.

A scan of that technology came back as she expected: they were designed through a similar path as their own work. More Orb knowledge adopted and adapted to fit the culture that the device was found on. Unfortunately, the planet's surface seemed to lack people but there were structures. When they had more time, Cassie hoped to be able to gather more data on them.

What we find down there may well hold the key to understanding what our enemy wants with the Orbs. We can only hope.

Cassie's heart skipped a beat when she broke through the static temporarily, only to be rejected by a large burst that hurt her ear. Wincing, she pulled off the headset and sighed, turning to look at the view screen. The battle outside looked chaotic. Small ships darted about and energy beams went in all directions.

The Gnosis was stepping into quite the mess.

"Open fire, Zach." Desmond's voice rang out over the low din of communication chatter. The pilot nodded once and acknowledged. A moment later, the Gnosis launched an attack, slamming the nearest enemy ship. Energy beams lanced out and connected, striking the rear. Their shields held and Cassie spun in her seat to get a scan.

Their defenses absorbed the energy, more of the fluid shield tech that she and Nathaniel had discussed. This was different than their first encounter. The data proved that they were facing a different classification of vessel, perhaps more combat oriented. Cassie turned to Salina who scowled at her own screen, intensely focused.

"No effect," Salina announced. "Shields are holding firm. If it helps any, they're holding against the drones as well."

"Interesting pick there, Zach," Desmond said. "You found the toughest one."

"And it's coming around," Zach replied. "I think they're preparing to engage."

"Do we have a scan of the weapons on that thing?" Desmond asked.

"Yes, sir," Salina put them up on the screen beside the vessel with amber lines drawn to the different hard points. "As you can see, they have the same type of ordnance we fought back on Earth and as such, our defenses should be able to hold."

"Good, they're not giants, they just have a good wall." Desmond stood. "Alternate fire, Zach. Mass drivers then energy and so forth. Try to confuse those shields and get through. Cassie and Salina, I'm looking for both of you to come up with another solution if the brute force one doesn't work."

"We're on it," Salina replied.

A newfound pressure landed on Cassie's shoulders and she started working faster, trying to remain calm. She had to figure out why the alien security protocols were so different from those they left on Earth. Interference from the destroyed ships played a factor, mostly because the signal strength was diminished.

Maybe if I can boost the signal by a lot. Cassie brought up an inventory of all their surveillance tools. The Gnosis originally planned on charting planets and studying stellar phenomena. That meant satellites and probes, either of which would be able to give her the extra jolt she needed to make her application work.

"Captain," Cassie called out. "Permission to launch both a satellite and a probe. They're going to help me get through all this interference."

"Granted," Desmond said. He was busy at Zach's station. The guns began to fire, and they spoke in hushed voices about the results. On the left side of her console, she prepared her tools to launch while on the right, she looked at the scans on the enemy vessel to see how the attack was going.

The alternation made a small difference. Where their first attack had no effect at all, they were certainly giving the enemy shields a beating. Unfortunately, the results were slow. After five passes, the enemy defenses remained strong at eighty-five percent. Desmond called out to Vincent to redirect the bombers.

"We'll deal with those defensive platforms later, we need to take this guy down." Desmond returned to his seat. "We'll alternate between bombs, beam weapons, mass drivers and missiles."

The enemy returned fire and the ship shook. Salina spoke in her typically calm voice, "Shields holding firm."

Cassie launched the satellite and probe, directing them deep into the heart of the battle. Hopefully, the enemies will consider them to be little more than debris. Neither of the devices were built for combat but they wouldn't really be a threat until they started to broadcast her signal. By the time they started doing so, it would likely be too late to destroy them.

Once she planted her application in their systems, they'd be sending information back to her and the boost wouldn't be necessary. A timer started, showing it would take just over five minutes for both devices to be in position. She thought about sending two more just in case but hesitated. Additional resources might look like some kind of attack.

This has to remain subtle for it to work.

She diverted her attention to the attack, trying not to hold her breath. The fact they were being shot at sunk in. No one on the bridge seemed particularly nervous about it but she knew they were mostly acting. They didn't have time to think about the fight in Earth's orbit but this one, they had ten hours to contemplate.

And everything they were facing, everything they did out there was unknown. Even with their intel and preparation, they were a lone ship so far from home, distance didn't even matter. Pioneers who had to fight for their lives not only against the enemy they anticipated, but an automated one without any remorse or even biologically sentient guidance.

Just do your job and focus on the task at hand. That's how you get through this and remain effective. Cassie took a deep breath and returned to her console, prepping her application to send. The moment the boosting devices activated, she would hit the button for an upload. Until then, she would be patient … and wait.

***

Heat sat in one of three shuttles plunging down toward the surface of the planet. Their escorts weren't considered to be enough for what was going on so a couple deck hands manned the turrets, prepared to take on the drones flying around out there. Scans indicated there were more flying around at the twenty-thousand foot range so they needed to be ready.

Their objective was not directly below the major battle but it was close enough that the shuttles had to skirt the action. They were going for a facility built into the side of a mountain, not unlike Gamma Alpha. Intelligence indicated there were automated defenses as well as drones in the airspace.

Captain Darren Gabriel commanded the mission from the Gnosis but he sent Lieutenant Colby Topper to lead on the ground. At the briefing, they decided the unit needed more firepower and an officer present in case they lost connection with Gabriel. Not to mention they might make first contact with a reasonable species.

Heat wasn't thrilled with the prospect. The lieutenant was a good man and knew his way around a fight but he was younger, lacking command lead experience. Before he came aboard the Gnosis, he served with Captain Gabriel and rumor had it they were close friends but beyond that, they didn't know much about Colby.

I guess we're about to learn a whole lot about the man. I hope it turns out to all be good.

What made it particularly strange was that Sergeant Major Jose Lopez was left aboard the ship. He was the better choice for leading a bigger mission. They didn't ask Heat for his opinion though so he kept it to himself. Jose didn't seem to mind but then again, he was a consummate professional and wouldn't complain openly.

The shuttle hit orbit and Heat allowed himself to smile. That meant they didn't get attacked while in space. Their power armor would allow them to perform a HALO jump but they had to be close enough for gravity to kick in. Until they reached the planet, the chances of a death they had no control over were high.

While the ship bucked around from the turbulence the others started pumping themselves up. Their weapons were at the ready and they stood in preparation of departing the ship. The two guys in the turrets, more security personnel than marines, would remain with the shuttle in a defensive capacity.

Heat checked his equipment one last time. His HUD showed all systems in the armor were operational and the tie-in to his weapon let him know the battery was fully charged and ready for action. As he focused again on the window, he saw beams burst from the turrets as the drones began their assault.

Patching in to one of the defensive consoles, Heat watched the fight take place from their perspective. The drones were fast as hell and the targeting computer wouldn't even try to pick them up. As the man tried to lead them they danced about in the air, moving erratically. They seemed more like insects than devices created by sentient life.

However, as maneuverable as they were, they didn't have the advantages in atmosphere they did in space. Wind resistance limited them but they still managed to peel off three full volleys on the shuttle. The thing tried to pull up but turbulence slowed it down for just a moment.

The turret tore into the drone's hull and ripped it apart, sending the debris scattering off into the wind.

Another drone nearly rammed the shuttle, getting so close that Heat made an executive decision to bail out. He ordered the marines to line up and disembark immediately. The doors opened and they started jumping. With two left, Heat's eyes widened as he saw a drone come around behind them.

He lifted his weapon and called for those in front of him to get down. Firing, he caught the drone right in the nose and he didn't stop firing until it caught fire. Billowing flames erupted on it and the shuttle pilot moved just before it crashed into them. The drone clipped their side as it went by and Heat hit the deck.

One of the others pulled him to his feet.

"Damage report!" Heat shouted. "How bad is this ship?"

"We'll be able to make it down," the pilot replied. "Especially if the rest of you jump and lighten us up. We're going to need some field repairs to get out of here though."

"You heard the man!" Heat turned to the last two men aboard beside the guys on the turrets. "Bail out. Good luck, pilot. We'll see you when this is over."

Heat jumped out of the ship and noticed that the other shuttles had also deployed their troops. Eleven marines in all went on the mission, a little overkill in Heat's opinion but the importance of the mission dictated the extreme action. As they plunged toward the ground, he noticed the drones were still flying after the shuttles, taking pot shots at them.

The turrets fought back but the shuttle Lieutenant Topper had been on took the full brunt of multiple attacks. The engines caught fire and the pilots ejected along with the turret men. A moment later the ship exploded. Now we've lost a ride and we've got men to pick up. This just became more complicated.

Their escorts seemed to be busy well above them, still holding off the drones that might've pursued them. They'd been negated quickly as helpful but perhaps they were keeping them alive long enough to get to the surface. Granted, there were fewer drones flying around the planet itself but the shuttles could've used the help.

Heat patched himself in to Lieutenant Topper. "Sir, did you see the shuttle?"

"I did. We were just on that boat a minute ago." Topper paused. "Our escorts got waylaid. We are some ten thousand feet from landfall, Gunnery Sergeant. When we land, we'll establish a perimeter and send out a search and rescue. Shouldn't require more than two men. I'm not reading any activity on the surface. The only action is up here."

Heat was about to respond but had to fire his weapon again, shooting at one of the drones. It flew close enough that the wake caused him to drift dozens of yards away. He caught his target on the side but didn't do any appreciable damage. They weren't attacking the marines anyway. They wanted the shuttles.

They must be programmed for vessels, not something so small as people. Heat checked his altimeter. Nine-thousand feet. For once, he wished he could fall faster. The odd thought made him smirk and he directed his attention down. Their situation may not have been expected but at least they would be able to continue the mission.

☐

Chapter 7

Nathaniel knew the Gnosis well and he understood what to expect from normal wear and tear. Simulations gave him a general idea of how systems would respond to combat damage but they didn't do justice to the real thing. When the first shots slammed into their shields, there were electrical shorts they didn't anticipate in places that shouldn't have been impacted.

Lights in the recreation area all went down and they lost door control for crew quarters. Nonessential, but troubling that such things happened. He assigned one of the junior technicians to look into it while he focused on the shields. They might not be able to match the way the enemy shields worked but he could manually adjust them as needed.

The first couple hits from the enemy gave him some data to make alterations to the emission frequencies. Nathaniel could make alterations to the hardness of the field, which was intended to block mass drivers. This didn't matter much against their current enemy who seemed to only use beam weapons.

While the hardened field definitely stopped the attacks, it drew more power from the reactors. Loosening up the frequencies from the emitters would prevent damage without taxing the defenses as hard. As he altered the system, he began to understand the liquid concept he and Cassie discussed before.

Reactive defenses meant more than simply automating alterations. It meant absorbing the attacks and responding to their strength. In order to respond quickly enough, the emitters would need to be altering their parameters on the fly. They'd need sensor equipment of their own and the AI to make the right choice.

They were nowhere near such an advancement but while doing the work himself, he began to understand how to make it happen. The next blast hit the ship and brought him sharply back to reality. Everything shook and he held tight to his console to avoid falling out of his chair. Damage report showed they caused minor hull damage from the concussive force of the attack.

Beam weapons shouldn't have concussive damage. Not the way we understand them. The damaged section was a supply area and no one happened to be there when it was hit. Still, the automated repair systems were already operational in that section but Nathaniel needed to understand what happened.

The fact they took that kind of damage defied his theory about altering the frequencies for energy weapons. Data from the attack showed that just as the beam weapon hit their shields, a secondary blast followed the path of the attack and battered the Gnosis. It seemed to only work if they were able to keep the beam in place for at least a few seconds.

Not much for the pilot to do about that but perhaps if we angled ourselves the moment they attacked, we could mitigate those.

Nathaniel sent his report up to the bridge and continued tweaking the shields. They threw him a curveball and luckily, it didn't cost them too much. He needed to be more cautious going forward, especially with relatively unknown weapons. They might not be so lucky the next time.

***

Desmond nearly fell off his seat when a blast shook the ship. Salina reported minor hull damage and gave a rundown of how the attack worked. Nathaniel's report supported her explanation and gave them all something new to worry about. The ships they fought near Earth did not use such weapons so there was no precedent.

"Zach, do you think you can angle the ship during attacks like that?"

Zach sighed. "I recommend everyone strap in at their stations. We'll be pulling off some heavy maneuvers to do so."

"Okay." Desmond turned to Salina. "Send a ship wide communication that everyone who can should get secure. Those who can't … let them know what to expect. Vincent, do we have a report from the marines or pilots?"

Vincent frowned. "I'm getting a report in now. One of the shuttles is lost and another took serious damage. There are drones down there. Raptor Squadron is engaged with them. They haven't taken losses but Three and Four have reported damage. Mustang is in the thick of it with the alien flyers. They're also contending with the drones so it's tricky."

"What about the marines themselves?" Desmond asked. "Did we lose anyone with the shuttle? Did the pilots make it?"

"All hands bailed out … but I haven't heard if they all survived." Vincent tapped at his screen. "They should all make landfall within the next minute."

Desmond rubbed his chin. "Cassie, we need to know what's controlling all those drones. Are these platforms solely responsible or could there be something on the surface? If we take out the rest of the platforms up here, do we free our people up from fighting the drones? Can you find out soon?"

"I'm nearly done with the satellite and probe venture," Cassie replied. "I'll start a scan now and compile the data."

"Perfect." Desmond turned back to the screen and narrowed his eyes. The other capital ships were turning their attention away from the platform and moving to engage the Gnosis. Scans indicated their opponents weren't as maneuverable so they might be able to lead them away and keep some distance during the brawl.

We have to buy the marines time to deal with their problems on the surface but more than that, we need to make it safe for us to secure the package. That means all of these ships need to be disabled, destroyed or routed. We need to crank up the pressure and really hit these guys hard.

"Where are we at with the bombers?" Desmond asked. "Are they nearly in position?"

Vincent nodded. "They'll begin their attack run shortly and are coordinating with Zach to ensure their attack syncs up with his. I expect them to deploy shortly."

"We're on it," Zach added. "I'm on com with them now."

Desmond leaned back in his seat. "Then take them out, Lieutenant Commander."

***

Rhino Squadron took from some of the bravest pilots in the entire Earth military. These individuals flew heavy bombers, vehicles loaded with dangerous ordnance that lacked the maneuverability of their smaller fighter counterparts. They were deployed for the destruction of facilities in massive areas or in this case, capital ships with heavy defenses.

Squadron Leader Nolan Caplan headed up the unit with Flight Lieutenant Micah Zane as his second. Charger Squadron, another fighter unit, provided cover for them but they maintained a loose escort. The drones and enemy ships flying around made the going somewhat difficult, even as the larger vessels made their way around the perimeter of the combat zone.

Nolan had been attached to the Gnosis since the project first began. Back then, the bombers were meant to take out debris and massive asteroids. The engineers described the destructive force of their bombs, each one carrying a more immediately destructive yield than the atomic ordnance of the past.

And they left a cleaner footprint so an area wasn't forced to endure lingering radiation for generations.

Rhino had performed bombing runs in simulations hundreds of times. They even fought massive ships but they had never actually dropped a bomb on a live target. The weapons had been tested on debris only and proven quite effective. How would they react to the alien shields? Nolan had a few thoughts.

The worst case scenario involved them having no impact whatsoever and the bombs simply being absorbed by the defenses. This was highly unlikely considering the sheer power being inflicted upon the enemy. However, during the briefing he had been told about the enemy's ability to absorb beam weapons.

It stood to reason they might be able to take even a heavy blow.

The bombs might overload their defense systems, knocking out the shields entirely and allowing the Gnosis to finish the job. Sheer, overwhelming burst damage may be more than they could take. As they tried to absorb too much at once, the feedback potential could annihilate their generators which led to the best case.

A full volley from Rhino Squadron may well take the ship out entirely.

Nolan didn't dare hope for such an overwhelming success. As they rocketed forward, he kept a wary eye on his scanner, ensuring that none of the enemies out in the field decided to attack them. None of their enemies understood their silhouettes yet so they had an advantage. If the aliens knew what Nolan's people represented, they'd redirect forces to intercept.

The bombers were armed with turrets for close protection. AI controlled them but they could be manually engaged from the cockpit. Training simulators saw every pilot work through running and gunning but it wasn't an ideal situation. Evasion maneuvers suffered and sixty percent of the time, the bomber was lost when the pilot had to multitask.

That's why Charger gave them a decent perimeter. Their commander, Squadron Leader Anna Jager, seemed like a reliable soldier. Nolan only met her two days before their maiden voyage but she came highly recommended to the crew. Ultimately, none of them were tested together, not in true combat.

Today, he'd find out if high command's judgement proved sound.

Zach's voice filled the cockpit, "Scans show you're nearly in position."

"Affirmative," Nolan replied. They were going to coordinate their attack, ensuring that the bombs hit just moments after an energy attack from the Gnosis. Mass drivers would follow and another bomber would hit them again. Rhino formed up in a staggered line so they could fire without having to maneuver into a good position.

"Okay, I'll count it off. Mass drivers firing." There was no sound in space but the shells from the Gnosis slammed into the shields, causing blue electricity to dance upon the surface. The enemy shot back, their energy beam connecting on the starboard side of the bow. Zach did what he could to angle the ship but it didn't happen fast enough.

The alien's shot brightened, turning white for just a moment before going dark. "You okay, Gnosis? What the hell was that?"

"We'll survive," Zach replied. "I'm going for my next attack. Count thousand one and deploy your first payload."

"Got it."

Beams blazed in the darkness of space from the Gnosis, again connecting with the alien shields. A thousand one. Nolan muttered before pulling the trigger. "First bombs away. ETA fifteen seconds." He watched as the ordnance rocketed away, their tails flickering purple and gold from thrust.

This could be it. His bombs connected with the enemy, flaring up in an explosive light so bright he winced and had to look away. Scans went offline temporarily. "Gnosis, I'm not getting a good damage read out. What do you have?"

As Nolan spoke, the Gnosis fired again and Micah called out his own deployment of bombs. The ship must've weathered the attack then. I guess none of my scenarios happened. They can't take too much of this punishment. Again, a blinding light filled the combat zone and the enemy returned fire.

More of their ships directed their attention to the Gnosis. Nolan's scanners came back online and showed fighters incoming. The bombs must've seriously grabbed their attention as they risked disengaging with the drones to come after them. Charger squadron rushed to meet them, obviously hoping to keep them occupied long enough to finish the bombing run.

"Damage report coming in," Zach said. "We're reading hull damage and engine issues. Fire two bombs each, all of you. I'm going to hit them with everything we've got before they take another shot. I'm—"

Com went dead as the enemy fired again, slamming into the same spot they'd hit earlier. Nolan risked a look, noting sparks dancing around a visible hole in the Gnosis hull. Damn it! That looks pretty bad! "You heard him," Nolan called to Rhino. "Fire immediately."

Twelve bombs rushed away from their ships, a dozen purple-gold lights challenging the stars in brightness. The first two were taken out by automated defenses, turrets turned to shoot at them. Ten made their mark and Nolan had the peace of mind to look away before they ignited.

The flash went on for a good five seconds before a different color filled the cockpit. Orange-red light erupted from the hull of the enemy capital ship, fiery bits flying away from the damaged port side. The Gnosis opened fire with a continuous barrage of mass driver ordnance. The shells tore through what was left of the alien craft, ripping it in half.

"Rhino, do you read?" Zach's voice came through a great deal of static. "Can you hear me?"

"We're here," Nolan said. "You okay?"

"Damage reports are still coming through," Zach replied, "but the target's eliminated. Redirect and go after the original target. The platform has to go."

"Understood. We're on our way." Nolan checked his scanner, noting that Charger was heavily involved in some pretty nasty dogfights. They were winning their fight but he noted that they had lost one of their number. I didn't even hear the mayday. This damn battle is really hosing our coms!

"Jager, you guys have that or do you need help?"

"We're okay," Jager replied. "You're on the way to the next target, right?"

"Affirmative, we're being redirected to the platform but if you need us …"

"We don't. If you continue your current course, you should be good all the way to the target. You'll have to deal with the drones when you get closer though, so be ready. We'll catch up when we can."

"Thanks, Charger." Nolan sighed. He kicked in his engines and changed course, directing the others to form up on him. The fight wasn't remotely over and they had quite a few objectives to pull off before they could claim victory. Depending on the next several minutes, the battle might be won or utterly lost.

***

Salina rattled off an extensive but not insurmountable damage report. Desmond gritted his teeth as she went through the various systems that were having problems as a result of two heavy hits from the enemy. He turned to Cassie, drawing a deep breath before he asked his question. He didn't need to be snappy.

"How close are you, Agent?"

Cassie tapped her screen and pressed an earpiece harder against her head. "I'm … I'm in!" She shouted the last word. "I made it! Their security protocols didn't change and I'm able to access their com net."

"Lower their shields and turn off their weapons," Vincent said.

"I can't impact their systems that way but I can use my application to provide the sort of interference required to stop their weapon." She paused. "And I might be able to get coms too. It's working on that now. As far as the other question you had about the drones, the platforms are controlling them. However …"

Desmond sighed. "Yes?"

"There're other automated defenses on the planet's surface and those are controlled by something else … something inside the facility the marines are heading to." Cassie clicked her tongue. "Yes, the power's coming from the place where the Orb is stored."

"Protected, more like," Vincent muttered.

A brilliant flash of light filled the screen, whitening it out. Desmond stood up. "What the hell was that?"

Zach tapped his console and scowled at it. A moment later he let out a cry, throwing a hand over his head. "Contact down! We got him! That capital ship is dust!"

"Confirmed," Salina said in her typical calm tone. "The combination of bombs and alternate fire tore through the shields and finished them off."

"Excellent." Desmond felt a surge of relief fill his chest. "Good job everyone, but they're all converging on us now, right?"

"Four left," Cassie said. "And they're definitely coming fast."

Vincent leaned close. "If they have the same energy pile driver weapon, we might be in trouble, sir."

"Recommendation?"

"Let's fall back and move toward the planet. Give us some distance and lead them on a chase."

"We don't have the luxury of a prolonged chase." Desmond rubbed his chin, glaring at the screen. "No, we're going to attack. Cassie, when this fight starts, I want you to hit them with a burst of interference. Even if they don't use their weapon, we might be able to disrupt their communications. Messing with their coordination should help."

"Okay …" Cassie went to work.

"Get ready, Zach. Let them have everything we've got." Desmond looked down at the report. "Give them our Starboard side. Armor's holding better over there and I don't want them hitting the fragile side of the hull. Salina, are any systems actually down?"

"No, sir. But there are several decks that aren't safe to visit right now. Automated repair is still working to get the emergency fields online. Once they are, we can get in there and perform actual repairs." Salina paused. "Three people are in a serious condition. Other injuries occurred from what happened to the crew quarters."

Desmond sighed but nodded. "Understood. Engines are still one hundred percent and all weapons are online so we need to finish this up ... but without losing so much that we can't get home. Keep that in mind as we go forward, Zach. Set a course in case we have to pull away in a hurry. I'm willing to take a little risk but I want a back out plan."

***

Heat watched the ground rapidly approach. They were in mountainous terrain, with sheer rock walls to the north and massive boulders littering the area. He was aiming for something of a clearing, a path that led up the mountain. At some point in the planet's history, he might've been going for a road but the infrastructure was long since consumed by nature.

He ignited his retro rockets, slowing his descent. Five good bursts slowed him considerably but when he landed, he still sunk a good two feet into the dirt. The armor absorbed the impact. Energy blasts flew past his head and he returned fire, shooting at several targets up the path from him.

Are you serious? How? The enemy must've known where he'd land and rushed to meet him. He was hit in the shoulder before rushing to the left, moving toward a particularly large rock for cover. "Contact," he spoke into his com. "At least three targets. I'm under fire and have taken cover. Positions?"

"Coms are linked," Lieutenant Topper replied. "We're a good hundred yards apart. Converge on Sergeant Heathrow's position. Pinch the enemy as we go and we'll advance on the target from there. Confirm."

The rest of the men confirmed the order. Heat's HUD showed the others were on their way but he didn't have the luxury to wait. Moving to the edge of his cover, he aimed his weapon around, using the camera to get his bearings. Three enemies were exposed but he saw beams from at least two more positions.

So five … possibly six. I may not be able to get them all but those jack asses standing up … they're done.

Heat dropped to a knee and leaned out just enough to brace his weapon before firing. He missed his first target and the man tried to get out of the way. Heat quickly redirected and caught the guy in the head, blowing him back several feet. The HUD indicated life signals winked out on the target.

One down.

The rock all around him started chipping away. They began firing directly at his position, tearing through it enough to make him move back from the edge. Some of them shouted in some unknown language, one his men reported hearing when they went to relieve Gamma Alpha.

"I'm in position on the western side," Sergeant Gorman said. "Permission to engage."

"Granted," Topper said. "I'm in position to the east. Open fire."

Supporting fire erupted from behind and either side of Heat. He used his rockets to hop up on the embankment to his left, keeping low. For the half a moment it took to cover the distance, he was exposed and one of the aliens took a pot shot at him. It barely missed, slipping past his leg. As he landed, he crouched behind new cover.

The low rocks between him and the enemy provided reasonable enough protection and he didn't have to stand fully for a firing solution. Other marines converged on the area, pouring firepower into the alien position. Heat's HUD indicated they were breaking formation and dashing behind rocks.

Heat popped up and took aim, catching one of them in the back as he ran. The shield flared and saved his life, giving him a chance to dive to the left behind cover. Topper accessed their computers, marking various targets. The small squares represented the aliens and the large triangle indicated their destination.

No automated defenses yet. Perfect.

"Search and destroy," Topper said. "Kelly and Dorian, get angles and take point. We're taking these pricks down. Anderson and Vine, you're on rescue for the downed pilots. Sergeant Heathrow, I want you, Gillet and Gorman to move ahead and check on the facility. Get me some recon. Defenses, aliens and anything else of value. Camera shots and scans. Copy?"

"Copy, Lieutenant." Heat motioned for his men to follow him. "You heard the man. Let's make this happen."

Wreckage from the destroyed shuttle was nearly six kilometers away. The pilots popped transponders so the marines wouldn't have a hard time finding them. Luckily, the enemy was too occupied with their own activity to bother hunting down a couple of downed humans. If Topper's force didn't keep them pinned down, they might try to take the opportunity.

The mainstay of the marine force moved off while Heat and his men headed west. "We'll go roundabout to remain clear of the battle. Avoid engagement. Follow my mark."

They engaged their rockets, hopping over the uneven terrain and making good time. Weapons began firing to the east as the marines engaged the aliens. A small screen to the left of Heat's HUD showed the action. The battle took place near what appeared to be a landed shuttle. The enemy likely hoped to use it for support against the power armor.

When their turret lit up and started carving massive pieces of rock, the ploy worked and the marines were forced to temporarily withdraw. Even with their weapons and maneuverability, they didn't stand a chance against ship ordnance. Topper called for air support but Raptor reported the drones made an approach especially difficult.

They would have to turn to their own heavy ordnance, including small rockets and grenades. The good news was if the aliens were busy fighting the marines, they didn't have the opportunity to break into the facility to steal the Orb. Heat and his crew could grab their intel in peace. He planned on making the suggestion they go ahead and secure the device.

Providing they didn't encounter indigenous defense.

They cleared a rise and saw the facility for just a moment. A wide courtyard was covered by a rockslide and dust obscured all but the tallest structure. Sunlight gleamed off the exposed metal of the walls and a two story doorway sat atop a flight of destroyed stairs. They landed and crawled up to the top of the next hill, granting them a decent view of the area.

Heat's scans found several gun emplacements, all live and active. They'd recently fired as well and he caught sight of a dead alien body near the base of the stairs. "Looks like they tried to make a straight run for it just to see what would happen." There was a strong energy reading coming from inside and four turrets total. Each one had two barrels and were motionless.

"Tough approach," Gillet said. "Even from the rear, you'd be exposed for a good five seconds before you'd have any cover. And those doors. How're we going to get those open?"

"Help from the Gnosis," Heat replied. "I believe we've got a certified Orb genius aboard. We can put them to work."

Gorman gestured off to the left. "Sir, I've got movement over there. Looks like mobile defenses. Definitely not the aliens we've been fighting."

Heat saw it as well though it was obscured by a wall of rocks. It moved slow and deliberate, easily navigating the difficult terrain. He initiated a scan and identified it as a treaded vehicle following a set path. It turned and moved directly in front of the ruined stairs, giving them a good look at it.

It was roughly eight feet tall and ten feet long. Wheels were surrounded in aged, cracking treads which chewed up the dust and rocks but wouldn't last too much longer. Two gun barrels started near the back and hung over the front, putting them at probably eight feet each. A canister sat near the back, probably for missiles but it appeared to be empty.

The tank turned as it finished its pass in front of the building and disappeared behind the rocks. Though the marines and aliens were causing some real carnage not even two hundred yards away, this thing didn't seem to care. Its programming must've required someone to attack the structure to become activated.

"Probably won't be a problem with all of us," Heat noted. "It hasn't rearmed in a long time."

"Must be solar powered." Gorman gestured to the facility. "This place has been out of commission for a long time."

Heat checked his HUD to see how the battle was going. From the lieutenant's perspective, they were trying to get a good position to take care of the shuttle. Private Wheeler took some heavy damage to his armor and had to fall back. Private Bosh might've been dead. He hadn't replied to coms and his armor's sensors malfunctioned.

"I'm scoping a turret." Gorman interrupted his thoughts. "Two of them in fact. On either side of those big doors."

Heat squinted to see what he did and finally noticed the two boxes and something else: bodies. There were at least five alien bodies lying in the dirt nearby. A quick scan confirmed they were dead and that Gorman was correct in his assessment. "Good catch. They must still work. Do you see the corpses?"

"Wow … They went for it." Gillet shook his head. "But did the turrets do them in? Or that tank thing? How would they have gotten past it?"

"Maybe it's malfunctioning," Gorman suggested. "God knows how long it's been here … and how it's all screwed up."

"Sergeant Heathrow," Topper's voice crackled in his ear. "We need some support with this shuttle. Can you get here in a hurry?"

"We're on our way." Heat gestured with his head. "Follow me."

They had a good half mile to cover to get to the alien's position. Each man kicked in their rockets, hopping toward the destination. As they moved, Heat wondered about the single shuttle they were contending with. Unless the drones took down others, he didn't think the aliens would only send one. There must be more out there.

It didn't matter just then. The site came into view and at the apex of a bounce, he took a shot at the shuttle. His blast connected with the top but didn't cause any appreciable damage. As for the next one, they were close enough to see other targets. Aliens held up in solid cover they'd erected with some kind of stationary shields.

"Take those guys out," Heat said, firing the first shots. He connected with his target, a perfect headshot. Personal shields didn't stop that blow and the body hit the ground, unmoving. His men began firing, tearing into their ranks. Their moment of surprise allowed them to take down four enemies before they could react.

That's when Heat got an accurate count of their opposition.

Even with quite a few already killed from the battle, his scans indicated there were thirty more aliens to contend with. This was after the marines had fired rockets and used grenades on them and it didn't count the turret on the shuttle tearing through the rocky cover. Heat's computer stated that a direct hit from the cannon would be fatal.

Not a big surprise. It's meant to take down fighters.

They landed in cover with their opponents hardly forty yards away on the other side. Shouts in their strange language could be heard echoing off the cliffs. Off in the distance, they heard the boom of a ship's engines. Heat wondered if it might be their own air support or if the aliens finally got some assistance.

Anyone willing to fly around up there with those drones is insane or amazing. Heat risked a glance up but didn't see anything immediately. That didn't mean they weren't out there, flying their patrols with the patience of machines. The people who lived on that planet must've learned a lot about renewable energy to keep them aloft for so long and have them start out with enough of a jolt to gather additional sun.

"We're in position," Heat announced to Topper. "Four down … but it looks like we've got thirty to go."

"We're at a stalemate for a moment," Topper replied. "What did you learn about the facility?"

Heat filled him in on the doors, the bodies, turrets and tank. "It'll be a tough approach but we can manage. Providing we're not being shot in the back by these idiots."

"Understood. I'm still trying to get us some air support."

The ground shook from an explosion, some kind of frag grenade going off not even ten feet beyond their cover. Heat frowned. If the aliens were able to take out their cover, the fight would get chaotic fast. He took a quick scan of the topography, marking their next destination in case they needed to move. Gillet and Gorman confirmed.

Vine pinged them all. They found the downed pilots and were securing the area for evac. The men weren't in a good position to move so they were staying put. Topper confirmed their report but it was obvious he wasn't happy. The current fight needed everyone they could get. The other shuttle had landed safely but takeoff would be a nightmare.

Going through the drones a second time seemed suicidal, even if they flew low to help out.

Vine continued, "Scan data from the pilots confirms four alien landing zones for a total of five shuttles down here somewhere. Two are damaged and cannot fly but the other three should be able to take off. However, they're honestly just as stuck as we are with the drones."

"Thank you," Topper said. "I guess we can be grateful they're spread out. I'm done playing with these guys. Let's alternate attacks on that shuttle until we take it out. I've got visual. I'll call when the weapon is facing away from your position so you can attack without risking that cannon. Everyone sound off when you're ready."

This is going to be rough.

***

Cassie rubbed her eyes after staring at the screen for nearly five minutes without blinking. Her application operated on the alien's coding methodology so it should've been difficult to detect. After initiating the interference to disrupt their communication network, she kept a sharp eye on the application's logs for any signs of discovery.

Depending on their computer specialist's arrogance, they will either figure it out fast or not at all. They had a lot of time to study us before attacking Earth and we only had four days. Now I find out how good of students both sides of this conflict are.

The fact they broke into two forces instead of ensuring a victory on Earth gave her hope. They underestimated opponents. While they certainly believed the Gnosis to be a threat when they attacked Gamma Alpha, they didn't believe the defenses on the planet could hold them so long. Their tactics showed an impatient, raider like mentality.

They probably shouldn't have attacked this planet the way they did either but the brute force approach was working, albeit slowly. Whatever they hoped to gain from the Orbs must've been worth the expense of lives and equipment. What did they hope to gain? If only the prisoner wouldn't have died, they might've found these answers.

Piecing them together from what was happening at this new planet would be much more difficult. Depending on what they found when they took the Orb. Based on the reports from the surface, Cassie began to wonder whether or not anyone would be walking away with the prize. They weren't only dealing with the drones but other robotic opponents as well.

If Cassie had more time to study the drones, she might've been able to disrupt their signal as well but as she probed the signals coming from the platform, she found yet another deviation of the coding principles from the Orb. Everyone interpreted them differently enough to make them not immediately compatible but there were similarities.

Some of her colleagues had discussed the idea of there being a universal language in the Orb, a standardized computer practice far beyond their understanding. Even after countless hours and years of study, experts agreed they'd only barely delved beneath the surface. The prospect of securing a second Orb provided them with hope of speeding up their understanding.

Were they meant to be combined? Cassie began working on a theory that maybe they were all linked up through some kind of interstellar network. The prospect seemed impossible by their current standards but whatever species built the devices were clearly advanced far beyond anyone else in the galaxy.

She twitched when she heard something over her earpiece, something that she thought might be a voice. Boosting the gain and trying to clean up the signal, she heard additional syllables. More talk. The alien's language! Their com network, though diminished, was still functioning and she had tapped in.

"Captain!" Cassie cried out, engaging the translator she planned to use on the prisoner. "I've got their coms! They're weak but they're coming through!"

"Good job," Desmond replied. "Tell us what they're saying as soon as you know."

"Their formation is loosening up," Zach said. "But I'm picking up an energy surge and they're about in range."

"Beat them to the punch," Desmond replied. "Fire when ready."

Cassie went back to her application, recording the enemy com chatter and pumping it through the translator. A meter appeared showing how long it would take to finish the process. Tapping her foot impatiently, she directed her attention to the drones, noting they did not pursue the enemy beyond the orbit of the planet.

The automated defenses engaged the various fighters still flying around but they weren't leaving their perimeter. Perhaps they have a specific range from their platform before giving out? I hope there's something to study when we're done. All of this could be huge for our advancement but for now, we have to survive four to one odds.

Cassie sighed. I did not need to think about that just now.

☐

Chapter 8

Dennis Arden performed a flip, gritting his teeth from the pressure the maneuver applied to his body. The enemy fighter on his tail nearly collided with a drone and had to pull their own wild move to avoid it. Without a firing solution, his opponent went low and banked, trying to get back on his six.

The squadron leader climbed and gunned the throttle, heading straight for one of the capital ships that was moving away from the planet. His wingman told him to jog starboard just before firing a barrage at one of the enemy ships. A flash lit up the space behind Dennis and his scan indicated he was clear of the attack.

"Thanks," Dennis said. "I couldn't shake him."

"A drone took mine out," Shane replied. "Corey's down."

Corey Parks, Mustang Six, had lost his fighter. Dennis saw he'd ejected but with those small crafts flying around, he may well have been killed. They wouldn't know until the battle ended and considering what was going on out there, it didn't look like it was slowing down. The Gnosis took out the biggest of the capital ships but there were four more.

And their victory required quite the concerted effort. The bomber squadron was now on its way to the platform supposedly controlling the drones. If they could stop those things from causing trouble, the fight would simplify considerably. Dennis took several volleys from the little bastards and though they didn't have the power to take him out, they did some damage.

His left engine glitched out twice but seemed to be back on track and one of his stabilizers nearly got him killed when it didn't react instantly to a maneuver he needed. Luckily, his wingman had his back though he had to save Shane twice as well. Once from two drones attempting to ram him and another time from an enemy missile that nearly caught his tail.

They were able to shoot down the projectile ordnance so far but it was a risky trick to rely on. Dennis hoped Raptor would be able to join them but they were too heavily engaged with the orbital defenses that harassed the marine shuttles on their way down. They'd lost two ships during the fight and at least one of their pilots was confirmed dead.

Charger escorted the bombers so they weren't able to come to their aid either. If anyone doubted the superior talent of human pilots, they wouldn't after reading the after-action report from this conflict. Eighteen ships were more than holding their own against an overwhelming force. Academy pilots would likely study the battle for years to come.

If anyone was still alive to talk about it.

Dennis felt a surge of hope for a moment when his scanner brought back a lowball number of drones.

Less than twenty-five left. Unfortunately, the platform deployed another fifteen before he could even mention their good fortune to the rest of his unit. Couple that with the fact they still faced eighteen alien ships and they were in a rough spot.

This is the fight that never ends!

Charger reported heavy combat and Dennis frowned at the scan data coming through. Two of their ships received heavy damage and a third reported a random malfunction not related to the fight at all. Their targeting computer went down completely and they were on dumb fire mode for as long as they remained.

Automated repair didn't detect a problem so there was no fixing it mid-mission.

The Gnosis fell back from the major battle and brought the capital ships with it. This helped the fighters to not worry about turrets from the larger ships but it meant support was all that much further away. Dennis plotted a course back to them and noted it would take ten minutes at full throttle to catch up.

We're on our own for a while.

Two enemy ships disengaged from their drones and headed off toward Charger and the bombers. Dennis directed Shane to them and they altered course to follow, dodging drone fire and the debris of other ships along the way. Their path took them through some of the wildest fighting in the combat zone and even with evasive maneuvers, they took a small beating.

Shields were down to fifty percent when they broke from the swarm of drones and they were close enough to see the heat coronas of the fighters they were after. "Charger," Dennis said, "we're coming up on your position in pursuit of two targets. Please be advised not to shoot us. We'll be there momentarily."

"Understood," Jager replied. "We've got you on scans. Thanks for the assist. We're almost to our destination."

"Copy that." Dennis engaged his targeting computer and let it try to get tone but it continued to go for something to the left. He told it what ship to aim for but it ignored him. Damn it, mine too? The glitch seemed isolated but to experience it on another ship made him suspicious. Was the enemy doing something or did they have a systemic problem?

He informed Shane of what was going on.

"What the hell?" Shane sighed. "Looks like Hal's reporting the same problem."

"It might end up happening to everyone if we're out here long enough." Dennis switched to guns and used his reticle. He had a firing solution so pulled the trigger. Chunks of metal dashed away from him but only a couple hit the enemy ship. I need to get closer. He increased throttle, his body pressed tightly into his chair.

"Mustang One this is Charger One," Jager's voice sounded strained. "Please refrain from guns. You are flying directly into our path right now."

"Affirmative and sorry about that." He switched back to energy weapons and redirected his course, moving so he'd be firing at an angle away from his allies. Shane did the same, lighting up his target with several beam weapon attacks. The shields flared and the ship veered off. They stuck with the last one.

Dennis fired again, this time scoring a shot. His opponent flipped on a dime and came flying straight for him. He had to dive to avoid a collision and his computer screamed out an alarm for proximity. The brief moment passed and his heart raced as the enemy tried to get a solution on him.

Banking hard to the left, he came around and they played chicken once more, this time with gunfire preceding them. The enemy's beam weapon slammed into his shields, making the fighter shake but he scored a direct hit as well. Combined with his first assault, his target's shields dropped and something orange started spilling from the right side.

The fighter headed off toward the capital ships when they saw the pilot eject. A moment later, the ship exploded in a spectacular fashion. His buddy was nowhere to be seen. He'd bugged out completely but that didn't mean there weren't additional targets. Charger was facing some heavy resistance still and since they were already there, Dennis and Shane jumped in.

Drones swarmed the area, putting them into a defense hell of crazy maneuvers and desperate shots.

"We'll fill in with you guys," Dennis spoke to Charger. "Hopefully, we can get those damn bombers in position and get rid of these drones. There are fewer of the aliens now than us so they're going to redirect their efforts."

"Not for long," Nolan Coplan said. "We're thirty seconds from our deployment. In a few minutes, I'm hoping to see a whole lot of drones floating around out here with no further guidance. Stay tuned, folks. There's about to be a really big boom."

***

"Enemies are opening fire," Salina announced, still eternally calm. "Concentrated fire."

"Evasive!" Desmond gestured at Zach. The pilot slapped the controls and a half moment later, the ship jerked hard during the maneuver, nearly tossing people from their seats. A tiny shimmer indicated a shield graze but the beams seemed to fly right by. "Damage report. What happened?"

"Reports of minor injuries," Salina said. "Automated repair seems to have dropped offline when we pulled that maneuver but I'm rebooting it now. Should be back shortly. Other than that, we're good."

Desmond nodded. "Great work, Zach but we're going to have a lot more of that. Open fire, everything we've got."

Zach initiated an attack sequence, firing all their weapons at once. All at once, some of the lights dimmed temporarily and Desmond glanced back at Salina for an explanation. She held her hand up to buy a moment as she checked but meanwhile, the attacks found their mark, slamming into one of the smaller vessels.

Cassie took over for Salina, "Direct hit from the mass drivers, energy weapons and at least two of the missiles. It appears their automated defenses took down the rest of the volley. Their shields are … at … wow, thirty percent. They've experienced some hull damage from concussion. I estimate another solid hit like that would disable them at the very least."

"Gotta move," Zach grunted, working the controls like a concert pianist. The ship once again jostled the crew as it bolted to the side. This time, they didn't evade all the attacks and the ship shook violently from another blow. "Damn it!"

"It's okay," Desmond said. "Focus and return fire. Take that ship out."

"Minor damage in the hangar," Salina said. "Medical is reporting more injuries. The lights dimmed earlier due to the way we're manually regulating power to enhance the shields. If Nathaniel wasn't massaging them, that last hit might've caused more damage. In fact, it would've likely impacted our maneuvering thrusters."

"I'll be sure to thank him later," Desmond replied. He clenched his fists as Zach fired again, another full volley of everything they had. The lights didn't dim this time but he heard a strange zap to his left, like an electrical spark going off. "Did you hear that, Salina?"

Salina tapped her computer and grunted in annoyance. "Navigation circuit was overloaded but it's already switched to the secondary backup. I'm routing repair to the primary. Tertiary is still operational as well but I'd rather not rely on only one additional backup considering it's the only thing keeping us mobile."

"Direct hits," Cassie announced. "Shields have dropped … engines are no longer operational. That ship is done!"

"Initiate thrusters," Desmond said. "Full speed. Make us a moving target." He turned to his own screen and looked over the environment. The planet was nearby and a single natural satellite orbited it nearby. Rocky debris hugged the moon, acting as a curtain. More than a hundred tiny asteroids remained close together, a tight group held firm by gravity.

"We are at full speed," Zach reported.

Desmond hummed. He remembered something from the academy about targeting computers. They were fairly accurate and made combat a lot easier for the most part but they could get confused. Pilots flying smaller ships needed to take some manual control to pick their targets when more than one presented itself.

If they shared technology with the aliens, then there was a good chance they had similar limitations. The next decision he made might be the most dangerous but it would afford them a little breathing room in the fight with three other ships. Somehow, they had to even the odds without exchanging blows.

That wouldn't work out long term.

"Set a course for their moon," Desmond said. "Get us as close to those rocks as you can."

"Sir?" Zach said. "Those things are pretty close together. They look small from here but according to my scans, they range in size from our fighters all the way up to a scout … vessel … ah …"

Desmond smirked. "Very good. I'm glad you worked that one out." The ship shook from another blow to the rear. "Set course and get us there fast, if you please. We're slugging it out right now but that's not sustainable. We have to tip the odds somehow and giving them more things to shoot at seems like a pretty good idea."

***

Heat prepared himself to take his shots at the shuttle, waiting for the word to go. The cannon annihilated a boulder nearby, shards of stone flying in every direction. Topper called out for his team to go and the three of them popped up, firing their weapons into the stationary space craft.

Shields began to glow, absorbing the weapon's fire. Those are meant for ship to ship combat. There's no way we're getting through those with personal gear.

"Incoming!" Gillet shouted, gesturing behind him. Drones swooped in, strafing the ground around them before they could even move. High-pitched, rapid-fire blasts cut echoed off the rocks and distant cliffs. They didn't stop with the marines, sweeping over the shuttle as well. "What the hell? Why'd they suddenly decide to come after us?"

"We must be a credible threat now," Heat said. He got on the com. "Lieutenant, I recommend we fall back toward the facility and let these guys deal with the drones."

The cannon went off again and the drones came around for another attack. Heat and his men had to give up their position as their cover was trashed. They made a low hop to the next embankment and away from the attack. Coms filled with static for a moment and when they came back, shouting filled his ears.

"Cut the chatter!" Heat shouted. It took a second time to get them to calm down. That's when he noticed what had happened. Lieutenant Topper's life sign was negative. His last position put him in the vicinity of the last turret strike. Private Wheeler was with him and had also been cut down.

God damn it! "Listen up. I'm marking a rally point and I want everyone to make their way their now. Go!"

Heat marked an area between the shuttle and the facility. He wanted to remove the threat of the aliens before dealing with the automated defenses but that didn't seem practical. Besides, the drones were giving them cover now. They could focus on the primary mission and ignore the enemy.

It would've been better to just watch our backs and go forward. The Lieutenant got greedy attacking that shuttle. He wouldn't voice the thought but it might come out eventually anyway. The post-op briefing would definitely delve into the decisions made on the mission and considering they had already lost two men, one an officer, meant scrutiny.

The men arrived within a few moments and they were clearly rattled. Heat needed to get them back on track and focused on an achievable task. "We're going for the facility," he said. "This is what to expect: a small technical and two turrets. The vehicle has beam weapons but the missile canisters are empty. The emplacements are still active."

"What then?" Gillet asked. "Even if we take them all out, how're we getting through the doors? And what if those drones come back?"

"They're fast but our weapons can down them. I shot one when we were still on the shuttle." Heat pointed at three men. "Dorian, Kelly and Bosh, you're on air detail. The rest of you will on the lookout for alien interference while we try to get in the door. Those bastards are locked down by the drones right now but they won't be for long. Any other questions?"

No one spoke up. "Good, time's running short. By twos, get to the site. I'll take lead with Gorman. The rest of you follow and spread out. We're not taking any more casualties from splash damage shit. Now move!"

Heat initiated the first jump and headed back toward the facility. They were there in five boosts, back to the cover they took while gathering intel. The tank was on the far left behind a wall of cracked rock. Both turrets were closed up and the sound of battle back at the shuttle echoed eerily around them.

"Alright, tank first," Heat said. "Gorman, let's take down that wall and see if we can't give ourselves a little terrain advantage. Ready? Fire!"

They both took aim and blasted the rocks, aiming low. Dust exploded into the air as the top tumbled down. Some of the heavier boulders danced off the surface of the tank, clanging noisily. The cannons fired, blasting the offending stones while moving swiftly to avoid being buried.

While the thing survived the assault, it didn't come away unscathed. Massive dents occupied the top and the canisters that likely held missiles were totally crushed. It moved swiftly though, barrels swiveling on a turret as it scanned for enemies. The AI must've understood what such an attack meant and so it tried to locate a threat.

"Anyone with rockets left, give those treads a good blast!" Heat gestured. He used his targeting computer to get a lock and fired three of his own. They slammed home along with several others, dislodging one of the wheels. The vehicle stopped there but it turned in their direction and opened fire.

None of the marines were close enough together to give the vehicle a good target and as they sprung into action, they were able to keep moving fast enough to avoid the shots. Hopping from cover to cover, they kept out of its range while returning fire. Heat was about to give another order when someone leaped from the rocket and sailed straight for their target.

Gillet dropped two grenades on the target and fired straight down before he cleared it. When he hit the ground, he rolled, coming to a halt beside a boulder and out of sight of his unit. The grenades exploded, sending the tank five feet into the air. When it came down it landed on its side and teetered for several seconds before flopping over onto its roof.

A fire burned on the bottom and though the turret managed another shot, something blew within it. The debris went in every direction and a chunk of metal embedded itself a good six inches into a rock only feet from Heat's head. It might've had enough velocity to go through his armor but he didn't really want to think about it too much.

"Report," he called out. "Is everyone okay?"

"I'm good," Gillet said, waving from his position. Heat planned on having a talk with him later in private about the foolhardy maneuver but just then wasn't the time. Bosh was the only one who didn't immediately reply.

They found him lying down, life signs steady but he'd taken a shot to the leg. His armor was scorched but still attacked. "You're lucky you didn't lose that limb," Gorman said. "Can you walk?"

"My armor seems to be frozen up, sir." Bosh shook his head. "I'm trying to get the joints undone without getting out of the suit."

"Stay in there no matter what," Heat said. "The atmosphere here says it's okay but I'm not taking any risks." He got Vine on the com. "You guys okay?"

"Package still secure. We've got the shuttle and the men are all aboard. Do you need us over there?"

Heat considered it for several moments. It would be nice to get the shuttle in place quickly but the drones made it impossible. They'd have to cross the bridge of moving the Orb when they came to it. "No, stay where you're at. We're trying to infiltrate the facility now and when we're done, we'll need evac. Start thinking about how that'll work."

"Understood, sir. We're on standby."

Heat raised the Gnosis. He needed to give them the briefest update before proceeding with the mission. He was surprised when Commander Bowman's voice piped on the line. They're serious about this if he's in charge of the field op. "Commander, this is Gunnery Sergeant Heathrow reporting in."

"What've you got?" Vincent asked.

"Lieutenant Topper is KIA. We are proceeding on the mission. I've assumed command."

Vincent sighed. "Understood. Let me know if you need anything. How close are you to the objective?"

"There're only a few more obstacles to clear but we're almost there."

"Alright, soldier. I'll wait to hear from you. Bowman out."

Heat turned to the others. "Gillet, get Bosh out of the line of fire. As soon as he's in cover, let's pound those turrets and make sure they never open up again." He waited for his man to be clear of the combat zone then marked the targets, giving each man a designation through their HUDs. A green light in their helmets indicated it was time to shoot and they let loose.

Both turrets popped up the moment they took damage, spinning wildly to find a target. The marines attacked at enough distance that it bought them some time before the emplacements were able to zero in on their attackers. By the time they took aim, it was too late for them.

The left gun went first, fire bursting out of it like a cheap firework before the gun slumped in its encasement. The other one fired several shots, seemingly at random. Heat guessed they took out its targeting module. They all directed their fire and it slumped backward, hanging by a couple of wires.

"Scanning," Gillet said. "I'm not picking up any additional weapons here."

"Let's move." Heat led the way, walking instead of using the jump packs. He took the stairs three at a time, allowing his gun to lead the way. The sounds of battle continued in the direction of the shuttle, giving him some confidence that they still had a while to go before they would be attacked again.

They arrived at the turrets, checking them over to ensure they were truly destroyed. Both of them were smoking and one was in pieces. They'd done their due diligence in that regard. Heat had them bring Bosh over and helped him to sit up in some decent cover. Once he was secure, they turned their attention to the doors.

The monolithic entry towered over them with a panel on the left sticking out of the otherwise smooth surface. Heat and Gorman approached, looking it over. A number of lights flashed over the surface of what looked to be an input device and the wall itself was a screen with various characters spread across it.

Gorman spoke up. "This panel's been used recently. Look at the dust around the edges and how it's clean in the middle here and here."

"They probably tried it before the turrets tore them up," Gillet said. He gestured to the bodies. "These guys were too close to the weapons to get away easily. It would make sense."

"Doesn't matter one way or another," Heat replied. "Can you get us in, Gorman or do you need help from the ship?"

Gorman hesitated to respond, standing before the panel for a good twenty seconds. He finally shrugged. "I've run a scan but yes, I think I'll need some help. I'll get a line to the Gnosis right now. Watch my back, huh?"

"You heard him," Heat said. "We've got aliens and drones still out here. Spread out and take up positions. We're not quite done so don't relax just yet. I anticipate at least one more rush before we get in that door and God knows what happens when we're through. I'm not able to scan the interior of this facility so it'll be exciting."

"Yeah," Kelly said, "this trip has been so boring already, am I right?"

Some of the men chuckled, probably a much needed moment considering all they'd been through.

Heat smirked as well, turning his attention outward. When the attack came, he wanted to be ready and he didn't have to wait. The moment Gorman touched the panel, they heard a high-pitch sound in the air: more of the drones.

"Alright," Heat shouted. "Looks like the first fight comes from above. Aim high folks and get your asses ready. These things may not pack a hard punch right away but they shoot quick and there's plenty of them." A dozen black dots appeared over a rise, flying swiftly in their direction.

Well, shit. Heat dropped to a knee and took aim.

***

Cassie's station had two screens and she dedicated one of them to reports of the action going on outside. Mostly, she was concerned with how the Gnosis was doing. Their maneuver to get near the moon kept them moving fast enough to make them a difficult target and though the enemy had fired several times, they continued to miss.

Small favor there!

However, they'd be slowing down as they drew closer to all the rocks. Flying around those asteroids would likely be the most profound test of Zach's skills he had ever experienced. Cassie ran a private simulation and discovered that the medium sized chunk of debris would be enough to easily penetrate their hull and if it hit too hard, it could go right through shields.

"Banking," Zach said. "This will let us slide in near the moon and allow us to have forward facing fire on the enemies."

He's flying in backwards!? Cassie bit her tongue. The man spoke like he'd done it a million times and he sounded confident. No one else said anything so either they trusted him completely or they didn't know exactly what to say about it. Regardless, if it worked, she planned on buying him a drink ... and possibly a fruit basket.

Salina broke through her thoughts, announcing to the bridge, "I've mapped the paths of the different asteroids. They're in your console, Zach."

"Thank you," Zach muttered. "Yep, I'm matching speed of the biggest one ... and we're ... about ... there." The ship shook for a brief moment. "That was us skimming orbit. The moon's not that big but it's still got some pull. We're now moving amongst the rocks and I'll have to adjust speed in ... two minutes ... to avoid being hit."

"Excellent," Desmond said. "Distance to targets?"

"They're closing," Salina replied. "They'll have a firing solution ..." A blast erupted on the screen and narrowly missed them. "Now."

"Uh huh." Desmond shook his head. "Return fire, Zach. We should have the advantage now when it comes to targeting so hit them with everything you've got."

A communication came through on Cassie's terminal and she leaned toward her screen, boosting the gain. The enemy signal still ran strong and her translation device wasn't quite finished but this wasn't them. It came from the planet's surface. It took her a moment to clean it up and even when she did, static surrounded the words.

"This is Sergeant Gorman, requesting assistance. Do you read?"

"I read," Cassie replied. "This is Agent Alexander. What can I do to help? Do you need reinforcements?"

"Negative, I am at the facility which we believe to house this planet's Orb. I'm at a panel and I do not know how to get through. To make matters more complicated, we are under attack down here by drones. Can you assist?"

"Yes!" Cassie paused as the enemy's communications went silent. The feedback on her application indicated that they hadn't discovered it but something had gone wrong. It sent back messages suggesting they were no longer transmitting. A paranoid thought took her and she checked to see if the aliens had found a way into their systems.

Their network appeared to be clean and Cassie believed she knew what to look for. Of course, if I don't, there's not much I can do about it. She turned to the satellite she'd deployed and connected up to it, boosting her signal so she could help the marines. While it established a connection, she turned in her seat.

"Captain," Cassie began, "I've got some news."

"Go ahead."

"The marines have made contact with me. They are at the door to the facility and are requesting assistance getting in. I'm establishing a connection now. However, they are under assault by drones."

"Okay, that's partially great. It'll help when the bombers take out that platform." Desmond paused. "Was there something else?"

"Um … yes, I seem to have lost connection with the aliens. I was translating their communications but it suddenly went dark. I don't think they discovered it but to be honest, that's the only logical explanation."

Desmond sighed. "Understood."

"Direct hit!" Zach shouted. "I think their shields held though."

"They've taken out several of the rocks," Salina announced. "I'm recalculating the courses now … um …"

The ship shook violently and Cassie had to grab her console tightly to stay in her seat.

"What the hell was that?" Desmond asked.

"One of the rocks was sent off course by an alien attack," Zach replied. "It was moving fast. Shields held in that section. I'm altering our course and firing again. I might be able to finish this guy off in two more volleys but he's wily as hell. My first attack hit him hard but they're starting to throw themselves around out there. The ride for the crew must be terrible."

Cassie established a connection with the marine's computer and saw through his helmet on her secondary screen. There was a three second delay, which frustrated her. If only she'd deployed the satellite closer to the planet but that hadn't been its purpose. She needed it only to boost her ability to get the application sent to the ships.

"Okay, Sergeant. I'm seeing what you're seeing and running a scan." Cassie paused. "Tap the left hand corner twice. Note that we're on a small delay so wait for my response before doing anything else."

On the screen, she saw blasts hit the wall a few feet from Gorman. To his credit, he didn't even move let alone jerk around. That level of courage under fire came from nerves of steel. She put herself in his shoes and doubted she would've been so calm. The Gnosis crew sincerely impressed her.

"It's done," Gorman said. His voice transfer didn't seem to be experiencing a delay, which made it easier to offer support. "The screen's lit up."

A few moments later, Cassie saw what he described. The screen came online with text all over it. She turned to start her translator but paused, frowning at what she saw. Their opponents had got their first and already bypassed the security. Unless the inhabitants of that world used the exact same alphabet.

Cassie ran the already built text translator and smirked. They had gotten through and the application remained on the console. It was set to open the doors again in nine minutes and forty seconds. However, they did have an override. "Hit the bottom left of the panel then swipe to the right. When you're done, tap the upper right and hold it."

"Yes, ma'am."

"Another hit," Zach said. "Whoa! They're really returning fire now! And ..." Another hit on the ship made the lights flicker overhead. "One hit out of well over a dozen. However, many of the rocks around us have been destroyed."

"I've got the path for another group," Salina said. "Sent you the coordinates."

"We're on our way."

"When will these open, ma'am?" Gorman asked.

Cassie didn't have an answer but she knew they'd initiated the same sequence the aliens did. "I'm ... not entirely sure. But that's how they did it. I'm sorry I can't be more specific. However, you don't have to stay at the console anymore. You can get some cover and fight back until they open."

"Roger that," Gorman replied. "Thank you for the assist."

"They're almost through," Cassie said. "But the drones must be dealt with. It's getting hairy down there."

"Vincent, follow up with Rhino," Desmond said. Another blast took out one of the asteroids nearby. "Zach … our advantage is dwindling."

"I'm working on it, sir."

"Work harder. We have to even the odds before leaving this moon's orbit or we won't stand a chance."

☐

Chapter 9

Heat fired several shots before jumping out of the path of an incoming drone. It strafed the area he was just standing in, causing great plumes of dust and rock to dance in the air. He spun in place as he landed, firing at it as it banked to the right and moved for another attack vector. He missed and didn't have time to shoot again before the next ship came at him.

"Hey," Gorman's voice came over the com, "I spoke to the Gnosis and the doors should open soon. She knew how to get through."

"Great," Heat grunted, avoiding another attack. "Couldn't happen fast enough. How long?"

"I don't know specifically but I've got other news. The aliens made it in there after all."

"How the hell did they get past the turrets?" Heat took some shots at another drone, this time catching it on its side. When it tried to turn to avoid a cliff, the flap moved but it didn't provide it enough motion. Slamming into the rocks, it exploded, fire spilling down into the dust. "Those things were definitely still active."

"If they're in there, we can ask them," Gorman replied. "But ... oh shit!"

Their conversation ended as they both had to fight for their lives. If these drones are allowed to keep going, it won't matter if those doors open. We'll be long dead. Hurry up, you ancient alien tech pile of crap! Hurry!

***

Energy bolts flew past Nolan's cockpit, drones blasting away at him. His defenses fired back, catching one immediately and chasing others. The rest of Rhino Squadron was faring pretty well but the number of ships attacking them intensified the closer they got to the platform. Luckily, the automated ships didn't seem programmed to simply ram them.

Such a ploy would've been difficult to counter.

Vincent pinged him, "How close are you? The marines are getting hammered on the surface by these things and it looks like your platform might be the only thing left controlling them."

"We're nearly there but we have to get close," Nolan replied. "If we fire too far out, we'll give them plenty of time to shoot down our ordnance and that would end this run really fast. Believe me, no one wants this thing taken out more than me. They're all over us out here and Charger's got their hands full too."

"Increase speed if you can," Vincent replied. "Things are getting intense all over the place."

Nolan wanted to ask how the Gnosis was doing with their own problems but he couldn't afford the distraction. If they were in trouble, he didn't want to know about it in the middle of one of the most dangerous flights he'd ever engaged in. Even success might pull his mind in the wrong direction.

Best to stay focused on the target.

"I'm hit!" Flying Officer Red Halden called out. "Engine one is offline. Still operational … but I might slow down a bit, sir."

"Do what you can, Red." Nolan cursed internally. Their bombers were heavily armored and had fantastic shields. The drones clipped Nolan's ship a few times but they hadn't breached his defenses yet. If they were able to get through one of them, they must've hit him hard. Vincent wasn't kidding. We really need to move.

Their ordnance would make the target from their current distance but there was a lot of open space between them and the platform. These drones were quick enough to chase the bombs and take them out, with guns if not straight ramming them. Nolan felt like they needed to close the gap to at least half the distance they were at to ensure contact.

Maybe a couple shots would relieve the tension. Checking his payload, he still had four total bombs and if that proved true, most of his people would be around there too. Firing one wouldn't be a problem. Whatever they had left would more than annihilate their target and would likely be dramatic overkill.

"I'm firing my first shot," Nolan announced. "This is just to see if we can relieve the pressure, get these guys to chase a bomb instead of us. If they ignore it, we'll be firing en masse shortly so get ready." He depressed the trigger and felt the clunk below him of the bomb releasing from the vessel and rocketing off toward the platform.

The turrets chased several drones that went after it, each one taking shots, the streaking ordnance plunging toward their base. Their bombs were tough and it took quite a bit of punishment before they took out the engine. It continued to drift and Nolan accessed the remote detonation of the device, igniting it.

An orange ball appeared some distance ahead of him, taking out several of the drones at the same time. "Okay, so it did what I wanted but not what I hoped," Nolan said to the others. "We still need to close the distance. You saw how much. Go to full throttle. Charger, protect Rhino Six. He's not going to be able to keep up."

"We've got his back," Jager said. "But be advised, I'm down to four pilots and one of them has a busted stabilizer. This is nuts."

Understatement of the decade.

"Sir," Micah spoke up, "These beasts have a hard time with maneuvers at full speed. We'll have to disengage the safety protocols if we hope to pull up based on the distance we need to be at."

"I know … We can also start slowing down near the target zone." Nolan checked his scanner. "It'll take us nearly five minutes to get where we need to be at current speed. If we boost up, we'll be there in one and a half. The difference will be huge, believe me." Another drone strafed him and his turret took them out. Still, his shields dropped by ten percent.

"I see what you mean," Micah replied. "Let's do it."

***

Doctor Jason Holland had something just short of a crisis on his hands. The wounded from the ship poured into the medical bay. Their injuries ranged from minor to severe. A lot of burns from shorted panels but also concussion damage as well. With all the heavy maneuvers the ship kept taking, people were being jostled around who couldn't be strapped down.

The medical team themselves were suffering from it. Everything had to be lashed down like they were on a sailing ship from the old days. Jason sent an updated report of the people his team were tending to and let them know that no essential personnel had shown up yet. He felt like it might be a matter of time.

I'd love to see what's going on out there but I don't have the luxury. Are we in a situation where we're going to die at any moment? I can't think that way. Focus on the job, Jason. Just remain focused.

The patients in his care asked the same question in a variety of ways. There was fear but more frustration. Many wanted to get back to their posts but were sent by section heads. The dedication to their duties impressed the doctor but he saw why they were there. Most had been hurt too badly to continue to function at peak capacity.

Then again, maybe we should've left those who weren't hurt too badly behind. We'll need them to be performing their duties rather than sitting down here. For that reason, he discharged those who could perform the minimum requirements of their jobs and sent them back to work.

The rest who stayed truly could not function and the medical team focused on their needs. At least those who needed care would get it but just as he sent the last man through the door, three more entered. Jason sighed and sent up another report, letting the bridge know what was happening. I hope they wrap this up soon. We can't keep taking this kind of beating.

***

Nathaniel dispatched his team to various parts of the ship, coordinating them from his central control panel in engineering. They were keeping things together but would have a lot of work ahead of them when the fighting stopped. So far, the engines and hyperdrive module remained undamaged but they had to fix the hull damage before they left.

Luckily, the automated repair systems could get them to a point where travel was safe. If only they would be allowed to work for a while without another heavy blow undoing some of their work. Most of their problems came from different shorts throughout the system, strain they hadn't anticipated or at least planned for.

Rerouting power worked and Nathaniel had an entire list of systems to overhaul to prevent the problems from occurring in the future. They'd hoped to discover this stuff slowly, in a controlled manner. Combat certainly gave them immediate feedback, though not exactly how they'd like it.

In the back of his mind, he questioned whether they should've engaged the enemy. He took the required tactical courses to become an officer while at the academy so he understood Captain Bradford's rationale. The enemy was engaged with a hostile force and they could take advantage of that.

Still, it felt foolhardy. There were five large ships against their one. Numerous fighters. All the drones. A defensive platform and then a whole lot of unknown on the surface. Depending on how badly they were hurt at the end of the battle, Desmond would either get a commendation or a court martial.

I suppose I'm just in a critical mood since I'm seeing what every blow we take causes. Nathaniel's com started buzzing and he went back to coordinating his folks, putting aside his concerns. It wasn't his place to judge the command crew, especially when they had probably already survived the situation longer than they should've.

Time to have a little faith, I suppose.

***

Heat heard something scraping behind him, something that would've been ear shattering had it not been for the noise reduction technology in his helmet. Glancing back, his heart beat a little faster. The doors were opening but they did so at such a sluggish pace, he actually groaned. It would take half a minute to open enough for a marine to get through in his armor.

Perfect! Another strafing run battered his guys and he thanked whatever maker was out there that they'd be done with the battle in a few moments. That's when the doors stopped moving, freezing in place. "Gorman!" Heat shouted. "Get back to that panel and see what the hell happened! Get that agent back on the line! Now!"

He aimed skyward and fired at the incoming drones. They needed something to happen soon: escape or relief. Either one suited him just fine.

***

Desmond watched another of the enemy vessels list, their engines flickering out before their reactor sparked and exploded. The final two ships closed quickly, unleashing a constant barrage of fire at them. Most of the hits blew up rocks around the Gnosis but a couple got through, causing the emergency lights to kick in on the bridge.

Much of their cover had been scattered or destroyed. The Gnosis needed to get moving and though they had yet to fully even the odds, they were better off than they were moments before. Especially since the enemy seemed intent on charging them. That exhibited a level of desperation which led to mistakes.

"Full speed," Desmond said. "Play it like you're a fighter going for a rear firing solution. Salina, what's going on with the power? The lights specifically."

"Light controls shorted out in patches around the ship," Salina replied. "I've rerouted the power up here and engineering will take care of the rest. They'll be back up shortly."

The engines kicked on as they accelerated, taking a hard bank to follow the course requested. Zach watched his panel intently, bobbing his head as he counted something down. Desmond glanced at his reports, cursing at the number of injuries coming in. Those coupled with their damage meant they'd be out there for a while after the fight ended.

At least we've got the supplies for a stay.

More hits rattled the vessel as they passed under the enemy ships. Zach pulled them up, practically spinning as he did so. The maneuver made Desmond lean hard to the left against the force and he wondered how many people lost their footing from it. As they came around behind their target, Zach initiated a barrage of shots, tearing into the rear of the enemy ship.

Shields lit up and one of the engines went dark, sparking brilliantly. It veered, trying to turn in place while the other one accelerated and headed off away from both the Gnosis and the planet. They streaked away even as their comrade turned to fire. Zach hit them again, blasting away until more fire burst from hull damage.

"Is that ship fleeing?" Desmond asked. "Salina, do you have a vector for them?"

Salina shrugged. "I don't see anything to go to on scans."

"I hope they don't have backup out there," Cassie said. Her revelation made Desmond's stomach tighten up. If they did and could call them in, the Gnosis would not survive. "I'll keep an eye on it."

The enemy fired a few short bursts, splashing into the Gnosis shields. They shook but not nearly as violently as before. Unleashing another torrent of mass drivers, Zach blew through their defenses and ripped off the entire left side of the enemy ship. The remaining piece tumbled away, forced off by a sudden discharge of pressure.

Zach got them moving backward as the enemy reactor went up. The ship disintegrated a moment later, tiny bits of debris flying in all directions. "Enemy down!" The pilot shouted. "That's it! Just the guy who ran now!"

"What's he up to?" Desmond directed the question to Cassie. "Do you still have him on scans?"

"I do … I'm picking up a strong energy reading. Um … Salina, can you take a look? I'm not sure what that is."

Salina moved to her station and took a look. She shook her head. "They're going into hyperspace, sir. They're fleeing."

"We did it." Desmond sank in his chair, allowing him a brief moment to enjoy their sizable victory. "I want a full diagnosis and estimated time to repair. Meanwhile, Vincent, what's going on with the bombers? Have they finished yet? And the marines. We need to catch up with them as well."

"I'm on it, sir," Vincent replied. "Give me a moment."

***

Nolan was slammed into his safety straps as one of the drones hit him from behind. It didn't give itself enough time to escape before the turret took it down but the damage was done. One of his engines started acting up, fluctuating between on and off. He rerouted some power and gave himself an extra boost on his good engine, turning off the other.

The last thing I need is to blow up from secondary damage. He checked the distance to his target and noted they would be able to fire in less than twenty seconds. So damn close! I can practically taste the deployment.

"Get ready, everyone. Our moment's about here."

Someone fired a bomb early, the heat corona streaking in space. The drones went after it, firing wildly as they did. It nearly made the target before being taken out but the operator didn't detonate it. The ordnance did pull some of the enemy forces away but was ultimately wasted.

"Hold your fire," Nolan ordered. "That was close but we need to get all the way there. Focus, people and think. If we don't take this out, those drones will make it next to impossible to get our people off world. It's just a little longer."

Two drones flew into Nolan's path, heading straight toward him. They held their fire, seemingly intent on ramming him. His turret spun and opened fire even as he pressed the stick forward, bringing his ship into a slight dive to avoid them. The first erupted into flames and exploded but the turret cleanly missed the other.

It clipped his top, slicing straight through his shields and ripping the turret clean off his hull. His computer went crazy, warning him about the damage and mentioning hull breach. Automated repair put a forcefield up over the hole, a small one no bigger than someone's head. Nolan felt lucky to be alive.

Had he not made the decision to dive …

The drone that hit him was off his scanner. It must've destroyed itself. Great, so they can commit suicide to keep us away. That's going to make this even harder.

"You okay?" Micah asked. "That was insane."

"So far." Nolan checked their range. The optimal choice would've been another ten seconds but he felt they were close enough. "Deploy half your payload now. Keep some just in case we can get a little closer or have to make a second pass." The idea of another run made his guts ache with tension but these drones were wily.

Bombs launched from each ship in Rhino Squadron, streaking off into the darkness of space. They were spread out enough to avoid one destroying another from casual damage and as the drones tried to start chasing them, it became quite clear they wouldn't be able to take care of them all.

The first couple bombs were taken out but Nolan's scan showed they deployed fifteen. If Red was able to deploy in a few moments as well, that would add quite a few. I think we should go all out. "Everyone but Deanne, launch the rest of your ordnance. Go for it." More bombs filled the air, another fifteen heading toward their target.

"I'm here!" Red shouted. "Well … close enough! I'm firing!" Six more bombs joined the attack, these a bit late. They'd be tertiary fire if the station withstood the first two waves.

The drones went into a frenzy but they left the bombers alone. It was time to turn around and head back for the ship. Nolan gave the order and they spun around. His ship was lagging as the others passed him easily. Checking over his systems, the engines were flickering. Power was also inconsistent.

Losing the turret did far more than hamper his defenses.

"You okay?" Jager, from Charger asked him. "You're slowing down."

"They took off my turret in a suicide run," Nolan replied. "I'm having some system failures."

"I'm with you but um … look over your shoulder if you can."

Nolan complied, eyes widening as the bombs began impacting the surface of the platform. He held his breath, watching the massive explosions rocking the target. The drones didn't even manage to take out half the ordnance. He didn't have an opportunity to see the conclusion before his computer caught his attention again.

This message was far more startling: eject.

"I've got to punch out," Nolan said. "Jager, I'm hitting it now."

"You're on my tracking," Jager replied. "We'll bring you home."

Nolan jammed the lever down, gritting his teeth as he was thrown clear of his vessel in the tiny escape pod. Weightlessness followed … accompanied by silence. He started to spin and tried to engage the rockets to steady out. They didn't appear to work and as vertigo overwhelmed him, he felt consciousness ebb into darkness.

***

Heat took aim at a drone and prepared to fire, convinced that this one would perforate him. Gorman went to work on the door only a few moments earlier but that felt like a lifetime ago while under siege. The black triangle came around and began its attack run. The weapons lit up half a second before it should fire … when the engines suddenly stopped and it began to tumble. Heat's eyes widened as it sailed over his head toward the structure. "Gorman! Bounce to your right! Now!"

He saw Gorman flee the panel half a second before the drone slammed into the wall just above the door. It exploded, bringing the ancient stone down and with it, the door frame. Both collapsed into the dust with a ground shaking crunch. While that may have been the most dramatic end, other drones were dropping from the sky as well.

They hammered the cliffs and rocks all around them, exploding when they connected. Thank God, Gnosis or whoever finally took that thing out. I'm buying you a basket of bath products.

The marines converged on the downed door, aiming into the tunnel beyond. It was well lit with a tile floor blessedly free of dust. Something kept the place clean, probably more robots. Heat turned to the others, considering the situation. They had a great deal to take care of in short order.

First, with the drones down, the aliens would be free to move about again. They could be upon them at any moment. Second, Heat wanted the shuttle to be on the move to give them an extraction. Third, they had an injured man who couldn't go with them. His leg joint was fused from the attack he endured.

Bosh was lucky he didn't lose the leg.

"Let's fall back into the facility," Heat said. "Bring Bosh. We can hold that area easily enough against an incoming force. I'm going to call for some air support to get our shuttle here for extraction. Anderson and Vine will be here soon. Meanwhile, Kelly and Dorian will be on door detail. The rest of us are going to complete the mission."

Dorian hummed. "If they bring that shuttle with them, we're going to be in a rough spot. Especially with Bosh down."

"Not when Raptor gets here." Heat pulled up the pilots on his com. "Raptor One, this is Sergeant Heathrow on the surface. We require immediate and continuous air support. Do you copy?"

"This is Flight Leader Dimitri Gerrit. I'm afraid we lost Raptor One. We're on our way and should be over your position in the next couple minutes. Hold tight."

"There you go," Heat turned to the others. He raised Vine next. "Drones are offline. Anything preventing you guys from getting your asses over here in a hurry?"

"No, sir. We're on our way."

"Everything's coming together. Time to wrap this up and go home, guys." Heat turned and started down the tunnel. "Just follow me."

***

"Drones are down," Vincent reported aloud. "Rhino took down the platform and we're receiving reports that the drones are no longer fighting. They're just … drifting out there. We did it!"

"Hold off on that," Desmond replied. "Zach, get us back to orbit. I want a full report from the marines. If they need help, we're finally in a position to give it." He turned to Cassie. "Did you help them get through the door?"

"It was opening," Cassie replied. "But then we got into the final brawl and I lost contact with the surface. Too much interference. When we get closer, I'll definitely be able to check. I've got the protocols for their HUDs still."

Desmond leaned back in his seat and turned to the damage report. Nathaniel was estimating three days of repairs before they could leave the system. Supplies would easily hold for another month and longer if they took to rationing. He hoped it wouldn't come to that. Earth would assume they were dead after a week.

"Congratulations, sir," Vincent said, keeping his voice low. "That was an insane battle and you pulled it off."

"I wouldn't have even tried it if the planetary defenses hadn't already beaten down our opponents. Hell, we would've shown up to find ten of them here … or worse, they would've already looted the Orb and been gone." Desmond shook his head. "Frankly, I feel like I got lucky. It does seem that our focus on military tech won the day."

"At first, I considered their tech better but now I'm leaning toward simply different." Vincent shrugged. "Charger squadron reported some straggler fighters but they've been dealt with. We lost a couple of ships as well. I'm compiling the casualty reports now and should have them in the next half hour."

"Thanks," Desmond said. He looked at the view screen at the fast approaching planet. "When we arrive, have another shuttle deployed with marine reinforcements. They can help mop up and finish this op up. Allocate all available resources to repairing the ship. Get some strict adherence to shifts though. Exhausted people make mistakes."

"They're going to be motivated." Vincent started tapping on his screen. "Everyone will want to go home."

"That's why it'll be our job to temper their enthusiasm." Especially considering the cargo we'll have. I'm pretty sure that'll raise tensions a bit. Considering what these aliens were trying to do to get it, I'm feeling a little twitchy about bringing it on board as well. Or taking it home. We were a target worthy of a split attack before but with two?

Desmond shook his head at the thought and forced himself to consider the rest of the current operation. They had enough going on without worrying about the future too. He'd have plenty of time for that on the ten hour trip home and after everything he saw, he'd have a lot on his mind indefinitely.

☐

Chapter 10

Heat led the way into the hallway, moving to the left the moment he passed the fallen doors. The smooth floor was shiny and scans identified it as a type of manufactured metal. Light barely touched the apex of the arched ceiling, which towered nearly two stories above them. Whatever they needed to get inside that place must've been massive.

The hallway went on for nearly three hundred yards with the first set of doors fifty yards from the entrance. They'd have to cross the distance without cover but if something happened, there was enough height to make a hop possible. Heat set the doors as the first rally point and ensured his guys knew to stagger their line by ten feet, on the left and right.

Hugging the wall, his scanner picked up motion through a set of doors at the end of the area. Beyond that, a massive energy reading emanated from the center of the complex, which seemed to branch off a mile in each direction under the rocks. According to the scans, two main hallways made a plus sign in the middle and smaller corridors branched off.

If it was anything like Gamma Alpha, many of the rooms would be for research. Various offices would make up the rest along with lab space for researchers and technicians. He imagined the place used to be bustling with people all intent on devouring the knowledge they gathered from their Orb.

The lack of life made the place feel eerie, like an abandoned tomb.

"Sergeant Heathrow, this is Commander Bowman."

"Go ahead," Heat replied.

"I'm checking in. How're things going down there?"

"We're inside the facility marching toward the largest energy reading. I suspect it's their Orb. Be advised, there is an alien presence in here. They seemed to get the door open before we got inside."

"Okay. You've got some reinforcements on the way. They'll touch down shortly."

"Sounds good. Thank you, sir." Heat nearly reached the doors. "Is there anything else you need?"

"No, go ahead."

"Thank you." Heat set the connection to stand by and paused at the door, looking it over for any means of opening it. There wasn't a panel or any other protrusions indicating a method to access it so he continued down the line. They didn't have time to investigate anyway. The enemy still represented a credible threat to mission success.

Unless Charger took out their shuttle. Then the fight would essentially be over. The marines could sit back and starve them out if they had to. However, Heat fully intended to take the facility by force. No one knew how far away their base of operations might be. They could have reinforcements already on the way.

Moving further down the hallway, a firefight broke out up ahead. Someone shouted and a moment later, an explosion shook the floor. Heat scanned the area, specifically looking for a report on the structural integrity of the facility. He didn't want to be buried alive in there but it came back showing they weren't in any danger.

The place appeared to be built to withstand a serious bombing and even though it must've been ancient, something kept it up. Whatever robots maintained it were doing a fantastic job. Dust clung to the walls but the bones of the building remained strong. The notion of these automatons working after the end of the world felt eerie.

Everyone's dead but their legacy lives on in this monument to their technical successes.

"Contact!" Gorman kept his voice low despite the fact his helmet obscured his speech. "Non hostile I think."

A figure slipped out of the door at the end of the hall, watching behind him. He didn't notice the marines until he'd taken a good ten paces. They aimed their weapons at him and when he turned around, a cry of surprise tore through him and he threw his arms in the air and dropped to his knees.

"You … You are …" His English was heavily accented but easy enough to understand. His dark hair was cut short and his blue eyes seemed to glow in the low light. He was slight of frame, wearing a blue jumpsuit like the other aliens they'd encountered. "You are humans, yes? Soldiers of Earth?"

"Who the hell are you?" Heat asked. "Are you surrendering?"

"Surrender …" The word didn't immediately register but when it did, his eyes widened and he nodded. "Yes! I … Well…I was a prisoner of the Tol'An but I've escaped! They're pinned down, battling the turrets in an attempt to take the Trindisha. I very much suspect they will lose that fight."

"You didn't answer my first question."

"I'm … in your tongue … hm." The alien looked down in thought. "Ah! I am a Doctor. Researcher. Studier. Um … my name is Thayne Rindala."

"And why did these people capture you?" Gorman asked. "Or … whatever they did to bring you here."

"I am an expert on the Trindisha. I've dedicated my life to their study. I discovered the hive connectivity of them, how they communicate with one another and through that, I was able to determine their locations all across the galaxy. The Tol'An have been searching ever since but they are dangerous!"

Heat narrowed his eyes. "The ones outside won't be anymore. I'd like to believe your story but I'm afraid we're going to have to restrain you until you can be questioned."

"This I understand, much as I find it ... um ... regrettable? Yes. That is the word." Thayne held his hands out. "Please ... just keep me away from these fiends. They are murderers and worse! They must be stopped."

"Yeah, we intend to do just that." Heat gestured to the Doctor. "Gillet, take care of him. The rest of you come with me."

They advanced down the hallway past the doctor while Gillet cuffed him. The door remained open from where Thayne came from and they peeked in. Whatever fight was going on had stopped and a body sat not five feet away, lying on its back. Other Tol'An agents were blown to pieces here and there, making the scene absolutely ghoulish.

"What the hell did this?" Heat shouted back at Thayne. "What're we about to walk in on?"

"Automated defenses ... turrets in the ceiling and there was a robot vehicle in the center of the room but it has been dispatched. I think, at least. I broke free and ran as quickly as I could."

"Lovely." Heat sighed. He tried to scan the room but didn't come up with anything hostile. "I've got nothing. Gorman?"

"Same. Whatever's in there is obscured by some kind of interference."

The energy readings from what Heat assumed was the Orb started to mess with their instruments. It would only get worse before it got better. A distant rumble represented a ship coming close. There were too many options for who it could be so he brought everyone up on the com to ask.

"Who's here?"

"Our shuttle's arrived with Vine and Anderson. Raptor's also overhead now. We have air superiority."

"Thanks." Heat cast his gaze about the room, trying to determine where the turrets might fire from. The bodies had been blown to pieces so finding a specific vector was difficult. Without scans, he couldn't be certain either way and there weren't any holes in the floor. Only the bodies took the damage. "We have to draw some fire."

"I'll do it," Gorman said. "I can get across that room in a hurry and there appears to be cover on the other side."

Indeed, the room itself was mostly wide open but there were a few panels of what appeared to be computers here and there. If one hurried, they could get to the other side and press themselves against one of the metal cabinets. However, without knowing where the turrets were, it would be difficult to find protection there.

Heat said as much.

"What do you want to do then?" Gorman asked. "We have to get through here somehow."

"Why didn't you guys hack these things?" Heat shouted back again. "You got through the door readily enough."

"These are ... How do you say ..." Thayne really struggled to find the words. "Grid hop? Um ... Independent? No, no ... Oh! Off the grid! They are not on a network. They cannot be accessed remotely and their control systems are hard-coded into the devices. Only the original operators can get through their defenses."

"Why?" Gorman asked.

"Because they would have some kind of friendly beacon to keep them safe."

Gillet shoved past them and hurried into the room before Heat could stop him. Turrets from the four corners popped up and began shooting at him. He hopped about, using his jump jets in short bursts to increase his mobility. Heat was right about the cover, it wouldn't help and after a quick hop around the entire room, Gillet came back out the door.

The gunfire stopped. "There," Gillet said. "You know where they are now."

"Great work." Heat whacked him on the shoulder. "Not exactly what I was hoping but I guess I appreciate it." He turned to the others. "We know what to shoot now so I guess we do another hotfoot routine and take them out. I'll mark targets on your HUD and you guys start shooting. We need to make short work of these for whoever's out there."

"I'll do it again," Gillet said. "I've got the lay of the land ... so to speak."

"You're crazy," Gorman replied. "But good luck, man."

"Just don't miss." Gillet drew a deep breath. "Here I go."

Heat aimed at the far side of the room on the left. Gillet dashed forward and the turrets dropped again, unleashing a torrent of fire after him. The marines battered at the emplacements but by the time Gillet was nearly around the room, they didn't seem to do any appreciable damage.

"Cease fire!" Heat shouted, giving Gillet a chance to duck back into the room. "That ... didn't work."

"So glad I went out there then," Gillet panted. "What're we going to do? There's a bunch of bodies in there ... Looks like they tried to take these things down with force too. Also, I think I got hit on the shoulder ..."

Heat checked him over and there was a black mark where one of the energy blasts struck him along the way. At such close proximity, scans worked to indicate that the armor was still fully functional. It must've been a graze. He stepped away. "You'll be fine. You don't even need repairs."

"We can try rockets," Gorman said. "I've got two left."

"Anyone else?" Heat asked. No one spoke up. "I don't think this is a brawn situation. We need to figure out how to shut these things down, even if that involves busting some power lines or something."

A low hum came from the opposite side of the room, like a motor whirring up. They aimed their weapons through the door and Heat tried to scan it. Interference made it impossible and he cursed, contemplating their next move. Whatever that is won't be good and if we can't get by these damn turrets, what's next? Go around?

A wheeled robot rolled into the center of the room and began to police the alien bodies. Heat exchanged a look with Gorman who shrugged. "What the hell is that thing going to do with them?"

"Recycling, I believe," Thayne said. "It makes sense given the surprising lack of vermin and other creatures in this facility. We didn't find any organic tissue in the area so we assumed they must keep the place very clean. Sterile in fact."

"Lovely ..." Heat hummed. "We need another way around."

"We couldn't get through that door thing," Gillet said "No panels."

"Wait!" Thayne called out. "I can get you through the access ways. There's a trick to it, you see."

"And can we get to our destination through there?"

"Yes," Thayne replied. "The complex passages link up and form a continuous path. There's no incomplete paths. Er ... You call them...um...dead ends! That's it. Please, assist me with getting there. I will help."

"Release him," Heat said. "He's unarmed and wants to help, let's give him the chance."

Gorman didn't seem particularly pleased at the prospect but complied, helping the doctor up and taking the restraints off. The man immediately hurried over to the door they passed and swiped his hand along the edge of it. A square that had looked just like the wall began to glow green and Thayne drew a couple of symbols on it.

When he finished, the door slid open and he stepped back. "There you are. This is a normal office. The place we were attempting to cross was a major control room. You should not encounter any stationary defenses but there may be additional automated response units. We did take care of one outside before making the dash in."

"How did you avoid those turrets at the door?" Heat asked. "They popped up the second we got too close."

"I figured out how to spoof them but it was too late for some of the Tol'An. They were overly eager to get at the door, despite my warning." Thayne frowned. "In any event, we should be able to advance now. Shall we get to the Trindisha? I'm of the opinion all of us would like to leave this very dead planet."

Heat stepped up and checked inside, noting there was nothing but a desk and another door within. He walked in and moved to the other side of the room. The door slid open as he approached, revealing a slightly larger office with more desks and a couple of blank monitors hanging on the walls.

"There are computers in here," Gorman said. "Hey, Thayne, do you think you can access them? Shut down the turrets or any other automated defenses?"

"That might be a good idea," Thayne said. "The Trindisha will not fit through these doors. We'll need access to the control room so we can get it out of here." He approached one of the desks and started tapping away at the surface. It lit up, coming alive as he worked.

Heat marveled at how the previous race that lived there used their technology. Common surfaces became interfaces, saving space and resources. He wondered how it worked but his curiosity was idle at best. Humanity might well have already been able to do such a thing but it made it no less interesting.

"Oh dear," Thayne said. "It seems that they truly wanted to keep that device here."

"What's wrong?" Gorman asked. "What did you find?"

"It seems that the automated defenses are the least of our problems at this time. They have a countdown ... A um...device...explosive? Is that what you call destructive items?"

"Wait." Heat joined him. "You're talking about a bomb. Where is it?"

Thayne gestured around him. "This facility, the entire building, it seems they've set it up to be quite the destructive device. If what I'm reading is accurate, then when it unleashes its fury, this will be a mighty crater. Large enough to be mistaken for a meteor strike of enormous magnitude."

"And you mentioned a countdown," Gillet said. "Mind letting us know how much time we have?"

"I'm converting to your time ..." Thayne frowned. "It's a very short period. Oh! Five minutes."

"Five minutes!?" Heat took a deep breath to keep his adrenaline down. "We have five minutes to get that thing out of here? How'd it start?"

"Apparently, the Tol'An started it when they tripped the defenses in the command center." Thayne shook his head. "This might be the end of the Trindisha ... All of them, in fact."

"What's that mean?" Gorman asked.

"If one is destroyed, we've theorized they would all shut down until one is repaired. We are unable to do so with our current technology so it would be the end of them." Thayne looked at Heat. "We must get it out of here."

Heat cursed. "Can you shut off the bomb?"

Thayne shook his head. "No, but I was able to stop the turrets. They are off. If we hurry, we should be able to get the Trindisha to the shuttle and away before it goes off. I estimate we will have approximately thirty seconds to reach a minimum safe distance."

"God damn it." Heat grabbed Thayne and dragged him to the door. He started a timer on his HUD. "Gorman, get back to the front and make sure the shuttle's ready to go. We'll put the Orb in one and everyone else in the other. Have them idling and ready to hit the thrusters. Gillet, you're with us. Move! Move!"

They rushed off to their tasks with Thayne and Heat bursting through the rooms until the researcher was panting and covered in sweat. They passed by other offices filled with various tech wonders but there was no time to admire them. The last door was stuck, halfway open, and Heat used his armor enhanced strength to shove it the rest of the way.

The glowing Orb stood before them in an empty, spherical room. He could've been in Gamma Alpha. The thing looked so similar to theirs, like a perfect copy. It was taller than them but supposedly, they weren't particularly heavy. Even so, Heat knew he would need Gillet's help to carry it back out.

Heat glanced at Thayne. "Do you need to disconnect anything before we grab it? If we rip it off of there, will we hurt it?"

"One moment." Thayne rushed over and examined the pedestal. He tapped something at two points around the edge and joined them again. "It's free! Grab it and we can get out of here."

The timer showed they had less than three minutes to get it out of there. Heat grabbed it from the side away from the door and Gillet lifted on his end. "Thayne," Heat said. "Get moving. Run as fast as you can to get out of here. We'll be doing the same so stay left. Understand?"

"Yes, I do." Thayne bolted from the room, seriously moving despite his apparent exhaustion.

Heat counted down from three and they lifted, the hydraulics in their armor complaining about the weight. They moved in tandem, picking up the pace as they established their rhythm. The timer ticked down just to the left of Heat's vision, filling him with a sense of frustration at having to carry the thing.

Even when they got out of the complex, they would still need to secure it to the shuttle. Time continued to play against them, even as they crossed the control room where the turrets were dormant. Rushing down the hallway, the light ahead gave Heat a sense of hope, even as the timer in his helmet showed they had only had two minutes left and thirty of those were reserved for flight time.

The remaining Tol'An forces had arrived and the sound of gunfire made Heat curse aloud. "Are you kidding me? They're back? These guys!"

"Welcome back, sir," Gorman shouted. "We've got the shuttle lined up to get this thing secure ... Jesus, it's bigger than I thought."

"Yeah, we need a magnetic grapple to get it far enough away from here to be properly loaded on." Heat set it down as carefully as he could and hurried aboard the shuttle. Gunshots glanced off the walls near his head. "Take those assholes out! We don't have time for this!"

He spun the tether and pulled out the hook, dragging it toward the Orb. By the time he arrived, Gillet had already rolled it on its side to give him access to the metal part the alien culture attached it to. The magnetics on the hook should've been enough to keep it in place without attaching it to any protrusions but he was pleased to find a fairly stable bar on the bottom.

Latching it through there, it gripped it tightly and didn't seem like it would let go easily. I hope this works. He brought the line back in so that the Orb was pressed hard against the back of the shuttle. "Get the hell out of here!" He shouted. "You have forty seconds to reach a minimum safe distance! Send us a rally point when you're there!"

The shuttle lifted off and the moment it was ten feet off the ground, it sped away, igniting the engines for a quick burn. Heat fired twice at an exposed enemy, catching him in the shoulder before turning to the other shuttle. He directed his men to follow and they rushed over to board. "Where's Thayne and Bosh?"

"They're with the Orb," Gorman called.

"Then go! Go! Go!" Heat shouted, grabbing the safety bar over his head.

The shuttle lifted off and hurried away, leaving the Tol'An behind to contend with the explosion. As the timer counted down, Heat watched it intently, praying they'd left in time. It went from twenty to fifteen ... ten to five ... He didn't know exactly how far away they needed to be for safety but the complex was already small on the horizon.

When the explosion went off, the sky darkened over the facility. Smoke plumed miles into the air and it only took a moment before they felt the turbulence from the blast. It rocked the shuttle, making them buck like they were on a carnival ride. The pilot called out a mayday, but somehow, he maintained control.

The violent motion lasted for a good minute. All visibility around them dropped to zero. Dust and smoke consumed the air, like the aftermath of an erupted volcano. They continued to fly to some rally point far from the carnage. Coms were down due to the explosion and they couldn't scan for the other shuttle.

I hope this was for something. Heat sat down finally, strapping himself in. After all that … What a mess.

***

Cassie witnessed the explosion on scans but the reaction from the others drew her attention to the main screen. A brown dot appeared on the surface, spreading out a good hundred miles in every direction. It didn't seem all that impressive from orbit but according to the sensors, it was a vastly destructive force.

"The facility …" Cassie whispered. "It's been … destroyed."

"How?" Desmond demanded. "What happened?"

"I … I don't know." Cassie tried to bring up more information but the area was so full of interference, she wasn't able to get any intel back. "Salina, are you having any better luck?"

"Negative. It appears to have been a high yield explosive device … Though I'm not picking up any radiation. It was not atomic but whatever they used certainly had a similar effect."

"Our people?" Vincent asked. "Do we have them on scan? Anything?"

"There's too much noise," Cassie replied. She hesitated as a thought dawned on her. The marines, the pilots … Everyone they sent might've died in the explosion. Considering the gravity of what she was about to report, she bit her lip. "The entire area's a dead zone right now. I'm not able to get any energy readings at all."

"Salina?" Desmond asked, his voice tense.

"I concur with Agent Alexander," Salina said. "Weather patterns suggest it will clear up soon but I don't think we should risk any ships even. Not when we'll be able to scan the area soon enough."

"Understood." Desmond stood and approached the view screen. Cassie turned back to her station and waited for a window she could use to scan the area, to bring anything up, any data at all that might reveal the fate of their people. Ground zero seemed to clear up first, the center of the blast being the facility itself.

The crater made her eyes widen. Whatever exploded left a hole roughly fifteen stories deep and it annihilated the hills around it, leveling them. The blast left no trace of the building at all and no technology appeared on her scans of the area. Anyone within ten miles would've been killed instantly, of that she was sure.

Rather than report that, Cassie continued to probe with her scanners. She needed additional data before she offered up even less hope for the soldiers. Winds cleared away the dust as a storm rolled in. Heavy rains battered the area, as if nature wanted to wash away the scar blemishing its surface.

Tech beacons began to ping them. Cassie sat up straight, trying to boost the signal until one of the shuttles came online. "I've got them!" She shouted. "One of the shuttles! Captain, it's … it's flying!"

"Salina," Desmond said, "bring them up on com."

"Working on it, sir."

"This is Shuttle Craft Omega calling Gnosis control, please come in, over."

"This is the Gnosis," Salina said. "Report your status, over."

"Mission complete," the pilot said. "The Orb is secure and we'll be heading back to the ship momentarily. Over."

The bridge crew cheered, Vincent clapping his hands in excitement. Cassie was too relieved to celebrate. Sinking in her chair, she felt as if she'd just run three miles at a full sprint. She couldn't believe the situation was over, that they'd succeeded and now had their prize. Once they repaired the ship, they could head home.

So we can figure out the next step in this new adventure.

"Shuttle Omega," Desmond said, "this is the Captain speaking. Thank you for your service and I look forward to seeing you when you land. Over and out." He turned to Salina. "Find out what casualties we're looking at. Vincent, coordinate with Nathaniel to get our repairs underway and Zach … establish a high orbit. Let's bring our people home."

☐

Epilogue

Desmond headed down to meet Salina and Cassie so they could talk to their guest, Doctor Thayne Rindala. He had received a full briefing from Gunnery Sergeant Heathrow and looked forward to having a chat with an alien who genuinely seemed willing to help them. Still, they kept him confined while they vetted him.

They couldn't be too careful out there in space.

Several people were killed during the mission, including two fighter pilots, two marines and some crewmen who found themselves too close to the hull during the battle. Others were injured but would pull through. Considering the odds, he thought it would be much worse but while they lost only a few lives, they took heavier losses on the equipment front.

One suit of power armor was almost useless, two were obliterated and then there were the starships. A bomber was totally destroyed and another needed a complete engine overhaul. Five fighters were total losses with three more requiring extensive repairs. The Gnosis itself required a heavy amount of attention.

Nathaniel estimated a day before they could take to hyperspace again and three more days for all systems to be normal. The hull damage required dry dock to clear up properly. Until then, they'd make it safe enough to travel. Considering the odds they faced, Desmond felt fortunate to have come away alive at all let alone with such a report.

Cassie and Salina were waiting for him as he arrived and together, they entered Thayne's room. He stood up as they entered, offering a sheepish grin. "Hello," he said. "I've met Agent Alexander … but not you two."

"I'm Captain Desmond Bradford." He gestured to Salina. "This is Lieutenant Gold, my science officer. We understand you offered a lot of help on the surface. I want to personally thank you for that."

"I was a prisoner of the Tol'An," Thayne explained. "Thwarting their plans suited me just fine."

Desmond nodded. "How did you find yourself in their influence?"

"I'm afraid I was stolen … er … You would say abducted, I believe. They took me for my understanding of what you call the Orbs."

"And were you able to help them?"

"I had little choice. They threatened to kill me." Thayne sighed. "I hoped to delay them longer but when they arrived in Sol, I could no longer hold them back. Because your world was occupied, they believed they could take the Orb without needing me to break any sort of codes. But the other world … We knew it was unoccupied."

"And the drones?"

Thayne grinned. "I knew about them … but they did not. I located your Orb and the one you just claimed. I also was able to gather quite a bit of data about both places. The automated defenses may have been enough to drive them off … Unfortunately, it seemed they were more tenacious than I anticipated."

"Tell them how they felt about the defenses when they got there."

Thayne's shoulders slumped. "They were quite unhappy with me. One of them nearly shot me in the head over the situation. If they would've known how to get into the facility, I'm quite certain I'd be dead. Fortunately for me, they did not and when we arrived, the rest of the automated defenses made slow but steady work of them."

"Do you know why they want the Orbs?" Desmond asked. "What's the point?"

"You already understand what wonders the Orb you possess has granted. Imagine when you double the output of power, learn how they created these devices in the first place and really get to the heart of the information available. With every one you have access to, you are able to gather more data, and with it, practical applications of their research.

"Long ago, they could be on different planets and provide the users with the benefits I just described but now, after so many years, they have lost contact with one another. They power the creations left behind … but no longer exchange information. Bringing them together not only grants a culture more knowledge but access to energy the universe has not seen in ... you would say a million years."

"Energy ..." Desmond turned to Cassie. "I know that it always seems to generate power, but I didn't know the Orb was a source. I thought it was just a storage unit."

"We've always known that it emanates power but it was decided long before I got involved that we wouldn't push our luck and try to tap into it." Cassie shrugged. "If someone made a mistake ..."

"I get it."

Thayne continued, "the Trindishas seem to be designed with flexibility in ... er ... mind? Yes, that's it. I believe they initially built them as a means to store data and discovered a higher purpose. Whole planetary populations might draw energy from one, as an example. But what other wonders do they house? We can only guess."

Cassie added, "Imagine what we can do with two of them."

"So your culture," Desmond said, "your ... your people ... they are not the Tol'An?"

"Certainly not!" Thayne spoke with such passion, Desmond was convinced he might spit on the floor. "They are a ... a subgroup of our people. Worshippers, if you will. They have extreme beliefs about the universe and who should be leading it. Believe me, their rule would not benefit anyone but themselves."

Desmond turned to Salina. "So we're dealing with a militant faction of their people. They can't possibly have the resources of an entire government, right?" He turned back to Thayne. "And they don't have an Orb."

"Actually …" Thayne rubbed the back of his neck. "The advantage they lost was me … but they do have one of the Trindishas. Before I was taken, they broke in and stole my people's. They are hunted, believe me … but they've been planning this for a very long time. I believe our two cultures would be great allies."

"That's some good news," Salina replied. "Depending on how many ships these Tol'An folks have, we might need them."

"Well, hold on," Thayne said. "You see, we would make good allies but do not assume such a task will be easy. I am willing to help, as much as I may, but considering our current losses, it may be a difficult sell to bring our people together. At least right away. There are challenges, you see … and Trindishas are not the only item of value in the universe."

"What do you mean?" Cassie asked. "What other things?"

"Oh, The Tol'An have been hunting artifacts in every backwater planet they can find. Remember, they care for technology and are desperate to acquire it. While the Trindishas are by far the most sought after items, they are at the top of a very long chain. Our own people have collected some pieces and have put them on display or studied them for that matter."

"I understand the desire," Desmond said, "but what's the point? I mean, beyond academics, what do they want with these items? Are they weapons?"

"In some cases. Weapons ... wonders ... utilities ... things to make space flight easier. Speed quicker. All things are possible out there." Thayne smiled. "This is why exploration appeals. There are not dead rocks and burning stars alone but fantastic creations waiting for discovery. People and places, monuments and artifacts ... dangerous and peaceful.

"And we, your race and mine, are not the only beings to contend with. Our kind has competed and worked with others ... many in fact. The Tol'An may be our most immediate threat but believe me, they will be stepping into the territory of other cultures who will not look kindly upon it. The Pahxin will likely take some of the blame."

"Are they hostile?" Desmond asked. "These others?"

"Some. Some far worse than the Tol'An." Thayne narrowed his eyes. "Some are peaceful and maintain neutrality. They have specialties, like all beings. You have entered a vast world, my friends. One I hope you are ready for and the swift course in navigating the complexities of it."

"This adds a spin to things," Cassie said. "But I think we're going to have to worry about that when we've had a chance to regroup, repair and restock. I'm afraid you'll have to come back to our world, Thayne. At least until we figure some things out. We have a lot to talk about, not the least of which being what we plan to do next."

"No one's threatened to kill me and I may be able to help." Thayne's brows lifted. "I have not been home in quite some time but when I return, I can introduce your people to mine. Collaboration will be important in the days ahead ... If we can get past their suspicion. That will be the challenge."

"Do the Tol'An know where other Orbs are?" Salina asked. "Is that the concern?"

Thayne's enthusiasm slipped and he looked away. "Yes. I gave them the location to three." His eyes lit up as he looked back at Desmond. "But the good news is they only sent the one force to collect them. It will be some time before they discover their failure. We have plenty of time in that regard."

"A ship escaped," Desmond said.

"What?" Thayne's mouth dropped open. "But ... I thought you destroyed them all."

"No, one of them dropped into hyperspace in the middle of the fight. So we may not have as much time as you think."

"Oh no ..." Thayne sat down heavily. "We must return to your planet as soon as possible then. Prepare them for war. Explain the circumstances. Connect with my people and hunt down the Tol'An so they cannot see their plan to fruition. I will do my best to be an ambassador in this regard but know that I commit myself fully to preventing their success."

Desmond looked at the others before speaking again. "I'm sure we'll welcome the help, Thayne. We'll have more time to become better acquainted when we drop into hyperspace but until then, I'll leave you in the capable hands of Agent Alexander and Lieutenant Gold. Oh, and ... welcome aboard the Gnosis."